ADVENTURE
STORIES

D0277851

KINGFISHER
An imprint of Kingfisher Publications Plc
New Penderel House, 283-288 High Holborn
London WC1V 7HZ
www.kingfisherpub.com

First published in paperback by Kingfisher 1991
2 4 6 8 10 9 7 5 3 1

A CIP catalogue record for this book is available from the British Library.

ISBN 0 7534 1009 5

Printed in India

2TK/0904/THOM/MA/80HIB/F

1TS/0904/THOM/MA/80HIB/F

ADVENTURE
STORIES

CHOSEN BY
CLIVE KING

ILLUSTRATED BY
BRIAN WALKER

KINGFISHER

CONTENTS

THE GOLDEN APPLES
OF THE SUN

RAY BRADBURY

"SOUTH," SAID the captain.

"But," said his crew, "there simply *aren't* any directions out here in space."

"When you travel on down toward the sun," replied the captain, "and everything gets yellow and warm and lazy, then you're going in one direction only." He shut his eyes and thought about the smouldering, warm, faraway land, his breath moving gently in his mouth. "South." He nodded slowly to himself. "South."

Their rocket was the *Copa de Oro*, also named the *Prometheus* and the *Icarus*, and their destination in all reality was the blazing noonday sun. In high good spirits they had packed along two thousand sour lemonades and a thousand white-capped beers for this journey to the wide Sahara. And now as the sun boiled up at them they remembered a score of verses and quotations:

" 'The golden apples of the sun'?"

"Yeats."

" 'Fear no more the heat of the sun'?"

"Shakespeare, of course!"

" 'Cup of Gold'? Steinbeck. 'The Crock of Gold'? Stephens. And what about the pot of gold at the rainbow's end? *There's*

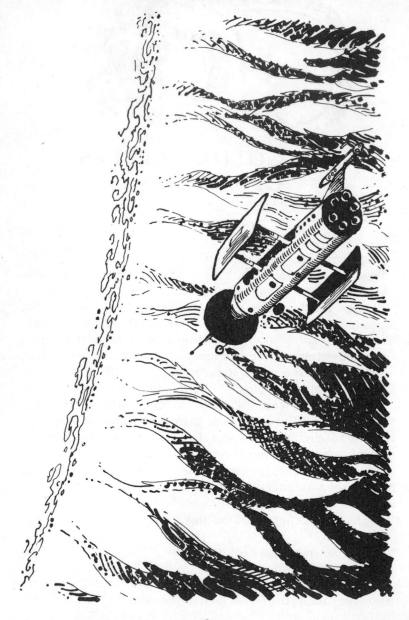

a name for our trajectory, by God. Rainbow!"

"Temperature?"

"One thousand degrees Fahrenheit!"

The captain stared from the huge dark-lensed port, and there indeed was the sun, and to go to that sun and touch it and steal part of it forever away was his quiet and single idea. In this ship were combined the coolly delicate and the coldly practical. Through corridors of ice and milk-frost, ammoniated winter and storming snowflakes blew. Any spark from that vast hearth burning out there beyond the callous hull of this ship, any small firebreath that might seep through would find winter, slumbering here like all the coldest hours of February.

The audio-thermometer murmured in the arctic silence: "Temperature: two thousand degrees!"

Falling, thought the captain, like a snowflake into the lap of June, warm July, and the sweltering dog-mad days of August.

"Three thousand degrees Fahrenheit!"

Under the snow fields engines raced, refrigerants pumped ten thousand miles per hour in rimed boa-constrictor coils.

"Four thousand degrees Fahrenheit."

Noon. Summer. July.

"Five thousand Fahrenheit!"

And at last the captain spoke with all the quietness of the journey in his voice:

"Now, we are touching the sun."

Their eyes, thinking it, were melted gold.

"Seven thousand degrees!"

Strange how a mechanical thermometer could sound excited, though it possessed only an emotionless steel voice.

"What *time* is it?" asked someone.

Everyone had to smile.

For now there was only the sun and the sun and the sun. It was every horizon, it was every direction. It burned the minutes, the seconds, the hourglasses, the clocks; it burned all time and eternity away. It burned the eyelids and the serum of the dark world behind the lids, the retina, the hidden brain; and it burned sleep and the sweet memories of sleep and cool nightfall.

"Watch it!"

"Captain!"

Bretton, the first mate, fell flat to the winter deck. His protective suit whistled where, burst open, his warmness, his oxygen, and his life bloomed out in a frosted steam.

"Quick!"

Inside Bretton's plastic face-mask, milk crystals had already gathered in blind patterns. They bent to see.

"A structural defect in his suit, Captain. Dead."

"Frozen."

They stared at that other thermometer which showed how winter lived in this snowing ship. One thousand degrees below zero. The captain gazed down upon the frosted statue and the twinkling crystals that iced over it as he watched. Irony of the coolest sort, he thought; a man afraid of fire and killed by frost.

The captain turned away. "No time. No time. Let him lie." He felt his tongue move. "Temperature?"

The dials jumped four thousand degrees.

"Look. Will you look? Look."

Their icicle was melting.

The captain jerked his head to look at the ceiling.

As if a motion-picture projector had jammed a single clear memory frame in his head, he found his mind focused ridiculously on a scene whipped out of childhood.

Spring mornings as a boy he found he had leaned from his bedroom window into the snow-smelling air to see the sun sparkle the last icicle of winter. A dripping of white wine, the blood of cool but warming April fell from that clear crystal blade. Minute by minute, December's weapon grew less dangerous. And then at last the icicle fell with the sound of a single chime to the gravelled walk below.

"Auxiliary pump's broken, sir. Refrigeration. We're losing our ice!"

A shower of warm rain shivered down upon them. The captain jerked his head right and left. "Can you see the trouble? Christ, don't stand there, we haven't time!"

The men rushed; the captain bent in the warm rain, cursing, felt his hands run over the cold machine, felt them burrow and search, and while he worked he saw a future which was removed from them by the merest breath. He saw the skin peel from the rocket beehive, men, thus revealed, running, running, mouths shrieking, soundless. Space was a black mossed well where life drowned its roars and terrors. Scream a big scream, but space snuffed it out before it was half up your throat. Men scurried, ants in a flaming matchbox; the ship was dripping lava, gushing steam, nothing!

"Captain?"

The nightmare flicked away.

"Here." He worked in the soft warm rain that fell from the upper decks. He fumbled at the auxiliary pump. "Damn it!" He jerked the feed line. When it came, it'd be the quickest death in the history of dying. One moment, yelling; a warm flash later only the billion billion tons of space-fire would whisper, unheard, in space. Popped like strawberries in a furnace, while their thoughts lingered on the scorched air a long breath after their bodies were charred roast and fluorescent gas.

"Damn!" He stabbed the auxiliary pump with a screw driver. "Jesus!" He shuddered. The complete annihilation of it. He clamped his eyes shut, teeth tight. God, he thought, we're used to more leisurely dyings, measured in minutes and hours. Even twenty seconds now would be a slow death compared to this hungry idiot thing waiting to eat us!

"Captain, do we pull out or stay?"

"Get the Cup ready. Take over, finish this. Now!"

He turned and put his hand to the working mechanism of the huge Cup; shoved his fingers into the robot Glove. A twitch of his hand here moved a gigantic hand, with gigantic metal fingers, from the bowels of the ship. Now, now, the great metal hand slid out holding the huge *Copa de Oro*, breathless, into the iron furnace, the bodiless body and the fleshless flesh of the sun.

A million years ago, thought the captain, quickly, quickly, as he moved the hand and the Cup, a million years ago a naked man on a lonely northern trail saw lightning strike a tree. And while his clan fled, with bare hands he plucked a limb of fire, broiling the flesh of his fingers, to carry it, running in triumph, shielding it from the rain with his body, to his cave, where he shrieked out a laugh and tossed it full on a mound of leaves and gave his people summer. And the tribe crept at last, trembling near the fire, and they put out their flinching hands and felt the new season in their cave, this small yellow spot of changing weather, and they, too, at last, nervously, smiled. And the gift of fire was theirs.

"Captain!"

It took all of four seconds for the huge hand to push the empty Cup to the fire. So here we are again, today, on another trail, he thought, reaching for a cup of precious gas and vacuum, a handful of different fire with which to run back up cold space, lighting our way, and take to Earth a gift of fire that might burn forever. Why?

He knew the answer before the question.

Because the atoms we work with our hands, on Earth, are pitiful; the atomic bomb is pitiful and small and our knowledge is pitiful and small, and only the sun really knows what we want to know, and only the sun has the secret. And besides, it's fun, it's a chance, it's a great thing coming here, playing tag, hitting and running. There is no reason, really, except the pride and vanity of little insect men hoping to sting the lion and escape the maw. My God, we'll say, we *did* it! And here is our cup of energy, fire, vibration, call it what you will, that may well power our cities and sail our ships and light our libraries and tan our children and bake our daily breads and simmer the knowledge of our universe for us for a thousand years until it is well done. Here, from this cup, all good men of science and religion: drink! Warm yourselves against the night of ignorance, the long snows of superstition, the cold winds of disbelief, and from the great fear of darkness in each man. So: we stretch out our hand with the beggar's cup . . .

"Ah."

The Cup dipped into the sun. It scooped up a bit of the flesh of God, the blood of the universe, the blazing thought, the blinding philosophy that set out and mothered a galaxy, that idled and swept planets in their fields and summoned or laid to rest lives and livelihoods.

"Now, *slow*," whispered the captain.

"What'll happen when we pull it inside? That extra heat now, at this time, Captain?"

"God knows."

"Auxiliary pump all repaired, sir."

"Start it!"

The pump leaped on.

"Close the lid of the Cup and inside now, slow, slow."

The beautiful hand outside the ship trembled, a tremendous image of his own gesture, sank with oiled silence into the ship body. The Cup, lid shut, dripped yellow flowers and white stars, slid deep. The audio-thermometer screamed. The refrigerator system kicked; ammoniated fluids banged the walls like blood in the head of a shrieking idiot.

He shut the outer air-lock door.

"Now."

They waited. The ship's pulse ran. The heart of the ship rushed, beat, rushed, the Cup of gold in it. The cold blood raced around about down through, around about down through.

The captain exhaled slowly.

The ice stopped dripping from the ceiling. It froze again.

"Let's get out of here."

The ship turned and ran.

"Listen!"

The heart of the ship was slowing, slowing. The dials spun on down through the thousands; needles whirred, invisible. The thermometer voice chanted the change of seasons. They were all thinking now, together: Pull away and away from the fire and the flame, the heat and the melting, the yellow and the white. Go on out now to cool and dark. In twenty hours perhaps they might even dismantle some refrigerators, let winter die. Soon they would move in night so cold it might be necessary to use the ship's new furnace, draw heat from the shielded fire they carried now like an unborn child.

They were going home.

They were going home and there was some little time, even as he tended to the body of Bretton lying in a bank of white winter snow, for the captain to remember a poem he had written many years before:

> Sometimes I see the sun a burning Tree,
> Its golden fruit swung bright in airless air,
> Its apples wormed with man and gravity,
> Their worship breathing from them everywhere,
> As man sees Sun as burning Tree . . .

The captain sat for a long while by the body, feeling many separate things. I feel sad, he thought, and I feel good, and I feel like a boy coming home from school with a handful of dandelions.

"Well," said the captain, sitting, eyes shut, sighing. "Well, where do we go now, eh, where are we going?" He felt his men sitting or standing all about him, the terror dead in them, their breathing quiet. "When you've gone a long, long way down to the sun and touched it and lingered and jumped around and streaked away from it, where are you going then? When you go away from the heat and the noonday light and the laziness, where do you go?"

His men waited for him to say it out. They waited for him to gather all of the coolness and the whiteness, and the welcome and refreshing climate of the word in his mind, and they saw him settle the word, like a bit of ice cream, in his mouth, rolling it gently.

"There's only one direction in space from here on out," he said at last.

They waited. They waited as the ship moved swiftly into cold darkness away from the light.

"North," murmured the captain. "North."

And they all smiled, as if a wind had come up suddenly in the middle of a hot afternoon.

POLLUX BOXES
WITH KING AMYCUS

ROBERT GRAVES

Jason and the Argonauts have set out from ancient Greece on the quest for the Golden Fleece. This is one of the adventures they have on their way.

UPON MAKING Cape Poseidon, the Argonauts shaped their course for the north-west, lowering the sail and taking to their oars. The high hills sheltered them from the wind, but they had not yet recovered from their exertions of the previous day, and their progress along the steep and rocky coast was therefore slow.

They rowed on for another few miles, until the coast took a westerly turn and the hills receded; then they came up with a prosperous-looking town, where herds grazed on rich meadow grass and a bright stream rushed down from the mountain.

"Does anyone know who these people are?" asked Jason.

Argus answered: "They are Bebrycians – or rather a mixture of Achaeans, Brygians and Mysians. Two generations ago an Achaean clan settled among the Brygians at the mouths of the Danube and inter-married with them; they later came here in a fleet of seal-skin rowing-boats accompanied by a number of Brygian fighting men, and soon subjugated the local Mysians. They are a strange people who prefer cow's milk to that of sheep or goats and mix their wine with fresh pine resin. I have heard that their King, who is nearly always at war with the Mariandynians and Bithynians to the north, is a savage creature named Amycus. He claims descent from Poseidon, to whom, in a style now happily abandoned throughout Greece, he offers human sacrifices on the slightest pretext."

Jason put it to the vote: "Shall we land here, or shall we row on?"

The decision was for landing, by thirty votes to two; so all put on their helmets and armour and, raising a defiant shout, beached the *Argo* opposite what seemed, from its size, to be a royal palace, and there made the hawsers fast to a fine bay-tree.

Echion the herald was the first to go ashore. He advanced with grave and fearless aspect towards the houses. A huge, shaggy, long-armed man with a squat head that looked as though it had been roughly shaped on the anvil with sledge-hammers – King Amycus himself, to judge from his golden ornaments – came out to meet Echion. But instead of greeting him with the formality that every man of honour shows to the herald even of an enemy, he bawled out roughly: "I suppose

that you know who I am. I am King Amycus. No, I do not want to know who you are or where you are bound – and no doubt your mouth is full of lies, in any case – but I would have you understand clearly how you are now circumstanced. No strangers are allowed to land in my kingdom, none at all. Once they have done so, whether by mistake or intentionally, they must accept the consequences. Either they may send out a champion to box with me, in which case I invariably kill him with my famous right-handed swing, or, if they prefer to waive this formality, they may shorten proceedings by an unconditional surrender. In either case, they are subsequently taken up to the top of the headland which you have just rounded and thrown splash into the sea as an offering to my great ancestor, the God Poseidon."

"I do not box myself," replied Echion suavely, "and I regret that Hercules of Tiryns, who was our shipmate until yesterday, is not aboard. He would have given you a pretty fair bout, I believe. Still, we have another champion of fisticuffs here, whom you may enjoy meeting. He is Pollux of Sparta, who won the All-Greece championship at the Olympic Games some years ago."

Amycus laughed. "I have never yet set eyes on a Greek who was of any use in the ring. I have, I own, seen Greeks do some very pretty boxing: with neat footwork, ducking and dodging in and out. But what does that profit them? Nothing at all, the fools! I always land my right-handed swing before long and it knocks them in a heap. They cannot hurt me, you must understand. I am nothing but bone and muscle. Hit me and break your wrist."

They went down together to the *Argo*, and Amycus shouted out in rude tones: "Where is this mad Spartan, Pollux, who styles himself a boxer?"

Jason said coldly: "I think that you must have misheard the words of our noble herald, Echion the son of Hermes. I am Jason of Iolcos, leader of this expedition, and I must ask you to address your words of greeting to me first of all."

Amycus uttered a contemptuous, bleating laugh and said:

"Speak when you are spoken to, Golden-locks! I am the famous and terrible Amycus. I trespass in no man's orchard and allow no man to trespass in mine. Before I pitch you all over the cliff, splash into the sea, one after the other, I wish to meet this All-Greece champion of yours and punch him about for a while. I am in need of exercise."

The Argonauts looked at one another in a wondering way, but by now the beach was thronged with the armed followers of Amycus. They could not hope to push the *Argo* off and get clear of the shore without heavy losses; and they did not wish to leave Echion behind in the hands of savages who could clearly not be counted upon to respect the inviolability of his person.

"Here I am, King Amycus," said Pollux, standing up. "I am somewhat stiff from rowing, but I shall be greatly honoured to meet you in the ring. Where do you usually box? Is it in the courtyard of your fine palace yonder?"

"No, no," answered Amycus. "There is a convenient dell under the cliff beyond the village, where I always fight, if you can call it fighting. Usually it is more like a simple blood-sacrifice."

"Indeed?" said Pollux. "So you favour the pole-axe style of boxing? Big men like you are often tempted to rise on their toes and deal a swinging downward blow. But do you find it effective against an opponent who keeps his head?"

"You will learn a good many tricks of the ring before I have killed you," said Amycus, roaring with laughter.

"By the way," asked Pollux, "is this to be a boxing match, or an all-in wrestling match?"

"A boxing match, of course," Amycus replied. "And I flatter myself that I am a true sportsman."

"Let me understand you fully," said Pollux. "As you may know, codes vary considerably in these outlying kingdoms. First of all: do you permit clinching, handling, or kicking? Or throwing of dust in the other man's eyes?"

"Certainly not," said Amycus.

"Or biting, butting, hitting below the hip-bone?"

19

"No indeed!" Amycus indignantly exclaimed.

"And only yourself and myself will be allowed in the ring?"

"Only we two," said Amycus. "And the fight is to the finish."

"Good," cried Pollux. "Lead on to the dell!"

Amycus led the way to the dell, which was a very lovely place, where violet, hyacinth, and anemone grew in profusion from the greenest turf imaginable, and the daphne scented the air. His armed followers took up their posts on one side under a row of arbutus-trees, leaving the other side free for the Argonauts. But on the way there, walking apart from the others, Idmon came upon a heartening augury: twin eagles perched upon the carcase of a shaggy black horse, newly dead, of which one was continually thrusting its head between the ribs to tear at the guts, but the other, already satiated, was wiping its curved beak against the horse's hoof. Other carrion birds, crows, kites, and magpies, were hopping and fluttering about, intent on sharing the meal. Idmon recognized the twin eagles as Castor and his brother Pollux, the eagle being the bird of their father Zeus; and the horse as Amycus, the horse being sacred to Poseidon; and the other carrion birds were Coronus, Melampus, Calaïs, Zetes, and the rest of the Argonauts.

"This is an unusual sort of ring," remarked Pollux. "It allows mighty little room for manœuvre. And both ends narrow to a point like the bows and stern of a ship."

"It suits my style of boxing," said Amycus. "And I may add that I always box with my back to the cliff. I dislike having the sun in my eyes."

"I am glad to know that," said Pollux. "In civilised countries it is more usual to draw lots for position. Come now, my lord, strip yourself, and bind on your gloves!"

Amycus stripped. He was as shapeless as a bear, though longer-legged. The muscles on his shaggy arms stood out like seaweed-covered boulders. His henchmen bound on his gloves for him – huge leather strips weighted with lead and studded with brass spikes.

Jason came striding forward to expostulate: "King Amycus,

this will never do! In Greece, studs of metal fixed upon gloves are forbidden as barbarous. This is a boxing match, not a battle."

"This is not Greece," said Amycus. "However, no man must be allowed to question my sportsmanship. Pollux is welcome to my spare set of gloves if he cares to borrow them."

Jason thanked Amycus, who ordered a slave to fetch gloves for Pollux of the same sort as those that he was wearing himself. Pollux laughed at the slave and shook his head, for Castor had already bound on for him his own supple sparring-gloves, which served to protect his knuckles from swelling and to brace his wrists. The four fingers of each hand were caught in a loop, but the thumb remained free and uncovered.

Jason whispered to Castor: "Why has your twin rejected those excellent gloves?"

Castor answered: "The heavier the glove, the slower the blow. You will see!"

The opponents agreed to begin the bout at the blast of a conch. The trumpeter took up his stand on a rock above the dell and was still pretending to untangle the crossed strings which attached the conch to his neck, when another conch sounded from among the crowd and Amycus rushed at Pollux, hoping to take him off his guard. Pollux leaped back, avoiding the right-handed swing aimed at his ear, side-stepped and turned rapidly about. Amycus, recovering himself, found himself standing with the sun in his eyes.

Amycus was by far the heavier man, and the younger by some years. Enraged at having to face in the wrong direction, he made a bull-like rush at Pollux, hammering at him with both hands. Pollux pulled him up with a straight left-handed punch on the point of his chin, and pressed his advantage, not with the expected right-handed swing but with another jolt from the same fist, which made his teeth rattle.

It took more than this to check Amycus. He ran in, head down, covering up his face against an upper-cut, butted Pollux in the chest and aimed a pair of flailing blows at his kidneys. Pollux broke away in good time and Amycus tried to pursue him into the shaded northern corner of the dell, where the sun did not annoy the eyes of either. But Pollux stood his ground and kept Amycus fighting at a spot where the sun would most trouble him: at one instant it was obscured by a rock and at the next it dazzled out again from above the rock, as Pollux stopped his rushes with hooks, jabs, chopping blows, and upper-cuts. Pollux fought now left-handed and now right-handed, for he was naturally ambidextrous, a wonderful advantage to a boxer.

After the contest had lasted for as long as it would take a man to walk a mile in no great hurry, Pollux was untouched except for a torn shoulder which, forgetting the spikes of Amycus's glove, he had flung up to save his head from a sudden swing; but Amycus was spitting blood from his swollen mouth and both his eyes were nearly closed. Amycus twice tried his pole-axe blow, rising on his toes and swinging downwards with his right fist; but each time he missed, and Pollux caught him off his balance and punished him, for he had drawn his feet too close together.

Pollux now began announcing in what places he intended to strike Amycus, and each warning was immediately followed by a blow. He disdained to strike any body-blows, for that is not the Olympic style, but always made for the head. He cried out: "Mouth, mouth, left eye, right eye, chin, mouth again."

Amycus roared almost as loudly as Hercules had roared in his search for Hylas, but when he began bawling obscene threats, Pollux grew angry. He feinted with his right fist, and with the left he landed a heavy blow on the bridge of his enemy's nose; he felt the bone and cartilage crunch under the weight of the blow.

Amycus toppled and fell backwards, Pollux sprang forward to strike him where he lay; for though in the friendly contests of the boxing school it is considered generous to refrain from hitting a prostrate opponent, yet in a public contest a boxer is considered a fool who does not follow up his blow. Amycus rolled over quickly and struggled to his feet. But his blows now came short and wild, his gloves seeming to him as heavy as anchor-stones; and Pollux did not spare the broken nose, but struck at it continually from either side and from in front.

Amycus in desperation snatched with his left hand at the left fist of Pollux, as it came jabbing towards him, and tugged at it, at the same time bringing up a tremendous right-handed swing. Pollux, who had been expecting foul play, threw himself in the same direction as he was tugged; and Amycus, who had expected him to resist the tug and thus fix his head to receive the swing, struck only air. Before he could recover, Pollux had landed a powerful right-handed hook on his temple, followed by a left-handed upper-cut on the point of his chin.

Amycus dropped his guard; he could fight no more. He tottered on his feet, while Pollux methodically swung at his head with rhythmic blows, like those of a woodman who

leisurely chops down a tall pine-tree and at last stands aside to watch it crash among the undergrowth. The last blow, a left-handed one that came up almost from the ground, broke the bones of his enemy's temple and knocked him stone dead. The Argonauts roared for wonder and delight.

The Bebrycians had kept pretty quiet during the fight, not believing that Amycus was being worsted. He had often before amused them by staggering about, pretending to be injured by an opponent, and then suddenly springing to life again and pounding him to a bloody pulp. But when Pollux began knocking Amycus about just as he pleased, they grew restive, fingering their spears and twirling their clubs. When at last Amycus fell they rushed forward to avenge him, and a flying javelin grazed Pollux on the hip. The Argonauts ran forward to protect their champion and a short, bloody fight ensued. Pollux joined in, just as he was, and showed himself as well skilled in the art of all-in fighting as he was in pugilism. He kicked, wrestled, bit, punched, butted, and when he had felled the man who threw the spear at him, with a kick in the pit of his stomach, he leapt upon him at once and gouged out his eyes. Castor stood over his brother, and with one blow of a long sword chopped a Bebrycian's skull clean through, so that one might have expected the halves to fall apart across his shoulders.

Idas, at the head of a small body of Argonauts armed with spears, ran along the lip of the dell and took the Bebrycians in the flank. They broke and fled through the arbutus-grove like a swarm of smoked-out bees. Jason, Phalerus, and Atalanta picked off the stragglers with arrows; Meleager pressed hard on the rout with his darting javelin. The Bebrycians streamed inland, leaderless and astonished, leaving forty dead or dying men on the field of battle; but Calaïs and Zetes pursued them a great distance, as kites pursue a flock of wood-pigeons.

Jason rallied his company, of whom three or four were wounded, but none seriously; Iphitus of Phocis had been knocked unconscious with a club, Acastus proudly displayed a spear-cut on the inside of his thigh which bled a good deal and made walking uncomfortable for him, and Phalerus had been bruised on the hip with a rock.

With one accord the Argonauts ran to the palace of Amycus in search of booty. There they found gold and silver and jewels in abundance, which they afterwards distributed by lot among themselves, and great quantities of provisions, including several long jars of Lesbian wine. Hercules had drunk the *Argo* nearly dry, so the wine contented them.

That evening, garlanded with bay leaves from the tree where the *Argo* was moored, they feasted well on tender beef and mutton; and protected themselves against a return of the enemy by arming some captive Mariandynians, whom

Amycus had taken in the wars, and posting them all about the town. But the Bebrycians did not venture to the attack.

Jason was deeply concerned not to offend the God Poseidon. The next morning, at his suggestion, old Nauplius of Argos, Periclymenus of Pylos, and Erginus of Miletos, all sons of Poseidon, joined together in preparing a sacrifice for their father. There was no lack of cattle, since all the herds of Amycus were now in the possession of the Argonauts, and what they could not eat they must necessarily leave behind. Making a virtue of necessity, they sacrificed to Poseidon no less than twenty unblemished bulls of the red Thracian breed, burning them utterly and not tasting a morsel, besides what beasts were sacrificed in the ordinary manner to the other gods.

That day, too, the Bebrycian dead were decently buried, King Amycus apart from the rest. The Argonauts did not fear their ghosts since they had died in fair fight.

Butes was delighted with a jar of wild honey that he had found in the private larder of Amycus: it was golden-brown in colour and culled wholly from the pine blossom of the Arganthonian crags. "Nowhere have I found so pure a pine honey as this," he declared. "The Pelion pine honey, so called, is tainted with a variety of other blossoms and flowers; but this has the authentic tang. Nevertheless," he added, "it is a curiosity rather than a delicacy."

SIR BORS FIGHTS
FOR A LADY

ROSEMARY SUTCLIFF

King Arthur's Knights of the Round Table each rode off alone on their quest for the Holy Grail. Sir Bors had vowed to fast on bread and water until he found it.

FOR THREE DAYS after parting from his companions of the Round Table, Sir Bors rode through the forest ways alone. And at evening on the third day he came to a tall, strong-built tower rising dark against the sunset, in the midst of a clearing. He beat upon the deep arched gate, to ask for a night's lodging, and was welcomed in. His horse was led to the stables and himself up to the Great Chamber high in the tower, full of honey-golden sunset light from its western windows that looked away over the treetops. There he was greeted by the lady of the place, who was fair and sweet to look upon, but poorly clad in a patched gown of faded leaf-green silk.

She bade him to sit by her at supper; and when the food was brought in, he saw that it was as poor as her gown, and was sorry for her sake, though for his own it made little difference, for he had taken a vow at the outset, that he would eat no meat and drink no wine while he followed the Quest of the Holy Grail; and so he touched nothing but the bread set before his place, and asked one of the table squires for a cup of water. And seeing this, the lady said, "Ah, sir knight, I know well that the food is poor and rough, but do not disdain it, it is the best we have."

"Lady, forgive me," said Bors, and flushed to the roots of his russet hair, "it is because your food is too good and your wine too rich that I eat bread and drink water, for I have vowed to touch nothing else, while I am on the quest that I follow."

"And what quest is that?"

"The Quest of the Holy Grail."

"I have heard of this quest, and I know you, therefore, for one of King Arthur's knights, the greatest champions in the world," said the lady; and it seemed as though she might have said more, but at that moment a squire came hurrying into the room.

"Madam, it goes ill with us – your sister has taken two more of your castles, and sends you word that she will leave you not one square foot of land, if by tomorrow's noon you have not found a knight to fight for you against her lord!"

Then the lady pressed her hands over her face and wept, until Sir Bors said to her, "Pray you, lady, tell me the meaning of this."

"I will tell you," said the lady. "The lord of these parts once loved my elder sister, never knowing what like she was – what like she is – and by little and little, while they were together, he gave over to her all his power, so that in truth she became the ruler. And her rule was a harsh one, causing the death and maiming and imprisonment of many of his people. Learning wisdom on his deathbed, and listening at last to the distress of his folk, he drove her out and made me his successor in her place, that I might undo what could be undone of the harm. But no sooner was he dead than my sister took a new lord, Priadan the Black, and made alliance with him to wage war on me." She spread her hands. "Good sir, the rest you must know."

"Who and what is this Priadan the Black?" said Bors.

"The greatest champion and the cruellest and most dreaded tyrant in these parts."

"Then send word to your sister, that you have found a knight to fight for you at tomorrow's noon."

Then the lady wept again, for joy. "God give you strength tomorrow," she said, "for it is surely by his sending that you are come here today!"

Next morning, Sir Bors heard Mass in the chapel of the tower, and then went out to the courtyard, where the lady had summoned all the knights yet remaining to her, that they might witness the coming conflict. She would have had him eat before he armed, but he refused, saying that he would fight fasting, and eat after he had fought; and so the squires helped him to buckle on his harness; and he mounted and rode out through the gate, the lady riding a grey palfrey at his side to guide him to the meeting place, and all her people, even to the castle scullions, following after.

They had not ridden far when they came to a level meadow at the head of a valley, and saw a great crowd of people waiting for them, with a fine striped pavilion pitched in their midst. And as they rode out from the long morning shadows of the trees, out from the shadow of the pavilion appeared a damsel in a gown of rose-scarlet damask mounted on a fine bay mare.

"That is my sister," said the lady, "and beside her, look, Priadan, her lord and champion."

The sisters pricked forward to meet each other in the centre of the meadow; and beside the damsel of the pavilion rode a huge knight in armour as black as his tall warhorse; and beside the lady of the tower rode Sir Bors, feeling the balance of his lance.

"Sister," said Sir Bors's lady, "as I sent you word last evening, I have found a champion to fight for my rights, in the matter between us."

"*Rights!*" cried the elder sister. "You played upon my lord when he was in his dotage, until you had wheedled him out of what is truly mine. These are your *rights!*"

"Damsel," said Sir Bors, "your sister has told me the other side of that story. It is she whom I believe, and it is she whom I will fight for this day."

And the two champions looked at each other, each searching out the eye-flicker behind the dark slits of his opponent's helmet.

"Let us waste no more time in talking," said Priadan the Black, "for it was not to talk that we came here."

So the onlookers fell back, leaving a clear space down the midst of the meadow, and the two champions drew apart to opposite ends of it, then wheeled their horses and with levelled lances spurred towards each other. Faster and faster, from canter to full gallop, the spur clods flying from beneath their hooves, until at last they clashed together like two stags battling for the lordship of the herd. Both lances ran true to target, and splintered into kindling wood, and both knights were swept backward over their horses' cruppers to the ground.

With the roar of the crowd like a stormy sea in his ears, Sir Bors was up again in the instant, the Black Knight also. And drawing their swords they fell upon each other with such mighty blows that their shields were soon hacked to rags of painted wood, and the sparks flew from their blades as they rang together and slashed through the mail on flanks and shoulders to set the red blood running. They were so evenly matched that it came to Bors that he must use his head as well as his sword arm, if he was going to carry off the victory. And he began to fight on the defensive, saving his strength and letting his opponent use up his own powers in pressing on to make an end.

The crowd yelled, and the lady he fought for hid her face in her hands. And Sir Bors gave ground a little, and then gave ground again, Priadan pressing after him, until at last he felt the Black Knight beginning to tire, his feet becoming slower, his sword strokes less sure. Then, as though fresh life was suddenly flowing into him, Bors began to press forward in his turn, raining his blows upon the other man, beating him this way and that, until Sir Priadan stumbled like a drunk man, and in the end went over backwards on the trampled turf.

Then Sir Bors bestrode him, and dragged off his helmet and flung it aside, and upswung his sword as though he would have struck Sir Priadan's head from his shoulders and flung it after his helmet.

When Sir Priadan saw the bright arc of the blade above

him, he seemed to grow small and grovelling inside his champion's armour, and cried out shrilly, "Quarter! You cannot kill me, I am crying quarter!" And then as Sir Bors still stood over him with menacing sword, "Oh, for God's sweet sake have mercy on me and let me live! I will swear never again to wage war on the lady you serve! I will promise anything you ask, if only you will let me live!"

And Sir Bors lowered his blade, feeling sick, and said, "Remember that oath. And now get out of my sight!"

And the Black Knight scrambled to his feet and made off, running low like a beaten cur.

And the elder sister gave a shrill, furious cry, and set her horse at the onlookers who jostled back to let her by; and so dashed through them and away, rowelling her mare's flanks until the blood on them ran bright as her rose-scarlet gown.

When all those who had come with her and Sir Priadan her lord saw what manner of champion they had followed, they came and swore allegiance to the lady of the tower. And so, with great rejoicing, she and her household rode back the way they had come. And in the Great Chamber of the tower, Sir Bors sat down and ate and drank at last, though still only bread and water; and the lady herself bathed and salved his wounds.

And after he had rested for a day or so, he set out once more on his quest.

THE PRISONER OF ZENDA

ANTHONY HOPE

Rudolf Rassendyll goes to Ruritania to rescue the imprisoned King, victim of the feud between the rival princes, Black Michael and Rupert of Hentzau. He is just in time to save the sick king from assassination.

IT WAS COME to the crisis now, and I rushed down the steps and flung myself against the door. Bersonin had unbolted it and it gave way before me. The Belgian stood there sword in hand, and Detchard was sitting on a couch at the side of the room. In astonishment at seeing me, Bersonin recoiled; Detchard jumped to his sword. I rushed madly at the Belgian: he gave way before me, and I drove him up against the wall. He was no swordsman, though he fought bravely, and in a moment he lay on the floor before me. I turned – Detchard was not there. Faithful to his orders, he had not risked a fight with me, but had rushed straight to the door of the King's room, opened it and slammed it behind him. Even now he was at his work inside.

And surely he would have killed the King, and perhaps me also, had it not been for one devoted man who gave his life for the King. For when I forced the door, the sight I saw was this: the King stood in the corner of the room: broken by his sickness, he could do nothing; his fettered hands moved uselessly up and down, and he was laughing horribly in half-mad delirium. Detchard and the doctor were together in the middle of the room; and the doctor had flung himself on the murderer, pinning his hands to his sides for an instant. Then Detchard wrenched himself free from the feeble grip, and, as I entered, drove his sword through the hapless man.

Then he turned on me, crying:

"At last!"

We were sword to sword. By blessed chance, neither he nor Bersonin had been wearing their revolvers. I found them afterwards, ready loaded, on the mantelpiece of the outer room: it was hard by the door, ready to their hands, but my sudden rush in had cut off their access to them. Yes, we were man to man: and we began to fight, silently, sternly, and hard. Yet I remember little of it, save that the man was my match with the sword – nay, and more, for he knew more tricks than I; and that he forced me back against the bars that guarded the entrance to 'Jacob's Ladder'. And I saw a smile on his face, and he wounded me in the left arm.

No glory do I take for that contest. I believe that the man would have mastered me and slain me, and then done his butcher's work, for he was the most skilful swordsman I have ever met; but even as he pressed me hard, the half-mad, wasted, wan creature in the corner leapt high in lunatic mirth, shrieking:

"It's cousin Rudolf! Cousin Rudolf! I'll help you, cousin Rudolf!" and catching up a chair in his hands (he could but just lift it from the ground and hold it uselessly before him) he came towards us. Hope came to me.

"Come on!" I cried. "Come on! Drive it against his legs."

Detchard replied with a savage thrust. He all but had me.

"Come on! Come on, man!" I cried. "Come and share the fun!"

And the King laughed gleefully, and came on, pushing his chair before him.

With an oath Detchard skipped back, and, before I knew what he was doing, had turned his sword against the King. He made one fierce cut at the King, and the King, with a

34

piteous cry, dropped where he stood. The stout ruffian turned to face me again. But his own hand had prepared his destruction: for in turning he trod in the pool of blood that flowed from the dead physician. He slipped; he fell. Like a dart I was upon him. I caught him by the throat, and before he could recover himself I drove my point through his neck, and with a stifled curse he fell across the body of his victim.

Was the King dead? It was my first thought. I rushed to where he lay. Ay, it seemed as if he were dead, for he had a great gash across his forehead, and he lay still in a huddled heap on the floor. I dropped on my knees beside him, and leant my ear down to hear if he breathed. But before I could there was a loud rattle from the outside. I knew the sound: the drawbridge was being pushed out. A moment later it rang home against the wall on my side of the moat. I should be caught in a trap and the King with me, if he yet lived. He must take his chance, to live or die. I took my sword, and passed into the outer room. Who were pushing the drawbridge out – my men? If so, all was well. My eye fell upon the revolvers, and I seized one; and paused to listen in the doorway of the outer room. To listen, say I? Yes, and to get my breath: and I tore my shirt and twisted a strip of it round my bleeding arm; and stood listening again. I would have given the world to hear Sapt's voice. For I was faint, spent, and weary. And that wild-cat Rupert Hentzau was yet at large in the Castle. Yet, because I could better defend the narrow door at the top of the stairs than the wider entrance to the room, I dragged myself up the steps, and stood behind it listening.

What was the sound? Again a strange one for the place and the time. An easy, scornful, merry laugh – the laugh of young Rupert Hentzau! I could scarcely believe that a sane man would laugh. Yet the laugh told me that my men had not come; for they must have shot Rupert ere now, if they had come. And the clock struck half-past two! My God! The door had not been opened! They had gone to the bank! They had not found me! They had gone by now back to

Tarlenheim, with the news of the King's death – and mine. Well, it would be true before they got there. Was not Rupert laughing in triumph?

For a moment I sank, unnerved against the door. Then I started up alert again, for Rupert cried scornfully:

"Well, the bridge is there! Come over it! And in God's name, let's see Black Michael. Keep back, you curs! Michael, come and fight for her!"

If it were a three-cornered fight, I might yet bear my part. I turned the key in the door and looked out.

*   *   *

For a moment I could see nothing, for the glare of lanterns and torches caught me full in the eyes from the other side of the bridge. But soon the scene grew clear: and it was a strange scene. The bridge was in its place. At the far end of it stood a group of the duke's servants; two or three carried the lights which had dazzled me, three or four held pikes in rest. They were huddled together: their weapons were protruded before them; their faces were pale and agitated. To put it plainly, they looked in as arrant a fright as I have seen men look, and they gazed apprehensively at a man who stood in the middle of the bridge, sword in hand. Rupert Hentzau was in his trousers and shirt; the white linen was stained with blood, but his easy, buoyant pose told me that he was himself either not touched at all or merely scratched. There he stood, holding the bridge against them, and daring them to come on; or, rather, bidding them send Black Michael to him; and they, having no firearms, cowered before the desperate man and dared not attack him. They whispered to one another; and in the backmost rank, I saw my friend Johann, leaning against the portal of the door and stanching with a handkerchief the blood which flowed from a wound in his cheek.

By marvellous chance, I was master. The cravens would oppose me no more than they dared attack Rupert. I had but to raise my revolver, and I sent him to his account with his sins on his head. He did not so much as know that I was there. I did nothing – why, I hardly know to this day. I had killed one man stealthily that night, and another by luck rather than skill – perhaps it was that. Again, villain as the man was, I did not relish being one of a crowd against him – perhaps it was that. But stronger than either of these restrained feelings came a curiosity and a fascination which held me spellbound, watching for the outcome of the scene.

"Michael, you dog! Michael! If you can stand, come on!" cried Rupert; and he advanced a step, the group shrinking back a little before him. "Michael, you bastard! Come on!"

The answer to his taunts came in the wild cry of a woman: "He's dead! My God, he's dead!"

"Dead!" shouted Rupert. "I struck better than I knew!" and he laughed triumphantly. Then he went on: "Down with your weapons there! I'm your master now! Down with them, I say!"

I believe they would have obeyed, but as he spoke came new things. First, there arose a distant sound, as of shouts and knockings from the other side of the *château*. My heart leapt. It must be my men, come by a happy disobedience to seek me. The noise continued, but none of the rest seemed to heed it. Their attention was chained by what now happened before their eyes. The group of servants parted and a woman staggered on to the bridge. Antoinette de Mauban was in a loose white robe, her dark hair streamed over her shoulders, her face was ghastly pale, and her eyes gleamed wildly in the light of the torches. In her shaking hand she held a revolver, and, as she tottered forward, she fired it at Rupert Hentzau. The ball missed him, and struck the woodwork over my head.

"Faith, madame," laughed Rupert, "had your eyes been no more deadly than your shooting, I had not been in this scrape – nor Black Michael in hell – tonight!"

She took no notice of his words. With a wonderful effort, she calmed herself till she stood still and rigid. Then very slowly and deliberately she began to raise her arm again, taking most careful aim.

He would be mad to risk it. He must rush on her, chancing the bullet, or retreat towards me. I covered him with my weapon.

He did neither. Before she had got her aim, he bowed in his most graceful fashion, cried "I can't kill where I've kissed," and before she or I could stop him, laid his hand on the parapet of the bridge, and lightly leapt into the moat.

At that very moment I heard a rush of feet, and a voice I knew – Sapt's – cry: "God! it's the duke – dead!" Then I knew that the King needed me no more, and, throwing down my revolver, I sprang out on the bridge. There was a cry of wild wonder, "The King!" and then I, like Rupert Hentzau, sword in hand, vaulted over the parapet, intent on finishing my quarrel with him where I saw his curly head fifteen yards off in the water of the moat.

He swam swiftly and easily. I was weary and half-crippled with my wounded arm. I could not gain on him. For a time I made no sound, but as we rounded the corner of the old keep I cried:

"Stop, Rupert, stop!"

I saw him look over his shoulder, but he swam on. He was under the bank now, searching, as I guessed, for a spot that he could climb. I knew there to be none – but there was my rope, which would still be hanging where I had left it. He would come to where it was before I could. Perhaps he would miss it – perhaps he would find it; and if he drew it up after him, he would get a good start of me. I put forth all my remaining strength and pressed on. At last I began to gain on him; for he, occupied with his search, unconsciously slackened his pace.

Ah, he had found it! A low shout of triumph came from him. He laid hold of it and began to haul himself up. I was near enough to hear him mutter: "How the devil comes this here?" I was at the rope, and he, hanging in mid-air, saw me, but I could not reach him.

"Hullo! who's here?" he cried in startled tones.

For a moment, I believe, he took me for the King – I daresay I was pale enough to lend colour to the thought; but an instant later he cried:

"Why it's the play-actor! How came you here, man?"

And so saying he gained the bank.

I laid hold of the rope, but I paused. He stood on the bank, sword in hand, and he could cut my head open or spit me through the heart as I came up. I let go the rope.

"Never mind," said I; "but as I am here, I think I'll stay."

He smiled down on me.

"These women are the deuce – " he began; when suddenly the great bell of the Castle started to ring furiously, and a loud shout reached us from the moat.

Rupert smiled again, and waved his hand to me.

"I should like a turn with you, but it's a little too hot!" said he, and he disappeared from above me.

In an instant, without thinking of danger, I laid my hand to the rope. I was up. I saw him thirty yards off, running like a deer towards the shelter of the forest. For once Rupert Hentzau had chosen discretion for his part. I laid my feet to the ground and rushed after him, calling him to stand. He would not. Unwounded and vigorous, he gained on me at every step; but, forgetting everything in the world except him and my thirst for his blood, I pressed on, and soon the deep shades of the forest of Zenda engulfed us both, pursued and pursuer. It was three o'clock now, and day was dawning. I was on

a long straight grass avenue, and a hundred yards ahead ran young Rupert, his curls waving in the fresh breeze. I was weary and panting; he looked over his shoulder and waved his hand again to me. He was mocking me, for he saw he had the pace of me. I was forced to pause for breath. A moment later, Rupert turned sharply to the right and was lost from my sight.

I thought all was over, and in deep vexation sank on the ground. But I was up again directly, for a scream rang through the forest – a woman's scream. Putting forth the last of my strength, I ran on to the place where he had turned out of my sight, and, turning also, I saw him again. But alas! I could not touch him. He was in the act of lifting a girl down from her horse; doubtless it was her scream that I heard. She looked like a small farmer's or a peasant's daughter, and she carried a basket on her arm. Probably she was on her way to the early market at Zenda. Her horse was a stout, well shaped animal. Master Rupert lifted her down amid her shrieks – the sight of him frightened her; but he treated her gently, laughed, kissed her, and gave her money. Then he jumped on the horse, sitting sideways like a woman; and then he waited for me. I, on my part, waited for him.

Presently he rode towards me, keeping his distance, however. He lifted up his hand, saying:

"What did you in the Castle?"

"I killed three of your friends," said I.

"What! You got to the cells?"

"Yes."

"And the King?"

"He was hurt by Detchard before I killed Detchard, but I pray that he lives."

"You fool!" said Rupert, pleasantly.

"One thing more I did."

"And what's that?"

"I spared your life. I was behind you on the bridge, with a revolver in my hand."

"No? Faith, I was between two fires!"

"Get off your horse," I cried, "and fight like a man."

"Before a lady!" said he, pointing to the girl. "Fie, your Majesty!"

Then in my rage, hardly knowing what I did, I rushed at him. For a moment he seemed to waver. Then he reined his horse in and stood waiting for me. On I went in my folly. I seized the bridle and I struck at him. He parried and thrust at me. I fell back a pace and rushed in at him again; and this time I reached his face and laid his cheek open, and darted back almost before he could strike me. He seemed almost mazed at the fierceness of my attack; otherwise I think he must have killed me. I sank on my knee panting, expecting him to ride at me. And so he would have done, and then and there, I doubt not, one or both of us would have died; but at the moment there came a shout from behind us, and, looking round, I saw, just at the turn of the avenue, a man on a horse. He was riding hard, and he carried a revolver in his hand. It was Fritz von Tarlenheim, my faithful friend. Rupert saw him, and knew that the game was up. He checked his rush at me and flung his leg over the saddle, but yet for just a moment he waited. Leaning forward, he tossed his hair off his forehead and smiled, and said:

"*Au revoir*, Rudolf Rassendyll!"

Then, with his cheek streaming blood, but his lips laughing and his body swaying with ease and grace, he bowed to me; and he bowed to the farm-girl, who had drawn near in trembling fascination, and he waved his hand to Fritz, who was just within range and let fly a shot at him. The ball came nigh doing its work, for it struck the sword he held, and he dropped the sword with an oath, wringing his fingers and clapped his heels hard on his horse's belly, and rode away at a gallop.

And I watched him go down the long avenue, riding as though he rode for his pleasure and singing as he went, for all there was a gash in his cheek.

Once again he turned to wave his hand, and then the gloom of the thickets swallowed him and he was lost from our sight. Thus he vanished – reckless and wary, graceful and graceless, handsome, debonair, vile, and unconquered.

SHANE

JACK SCHAEFER

Nobody knew where Shane came from when he rode along the trail to the Starrett's homestead. He makes friends with young Bob, and repays the family's hospitality by saving them from a threat to their lives and livelihood. But perhaps he is not so quick on the draw as he used to be . . .

NOTHING COULD have kept me there in the house that night. My mind held nothing but the driving desire to follow Shane. I waited, hardly daring to breathe while mother watched him go. I waited until she turned to father, bending over him, then I slipped around the doorpost out to the porch. I thought for a moment she had noticed me, but I could not be sure and she did not call to me. I went softly down the steps and into the freedom of the night.

Shane was nowhere in sight. I stayed in the darker shadows, looking about, and at last I saw him emerging once more from the barn. The moon was rising low over the mountains, a clean, bright crescent. Its light was enough for me to see him plainly in outline. He was carrying his saddle and a sudden pain stabbed through me as I saw that with it was his saddle-roll. He went toward the pasture gate, not slow, not fast, just firm and steady. There was a catlike certainty in his every movement, a silent, inevitable deadliness. I heard him, there by the gate, give his low whistle and the horse came out of the shadows at the far end of the pasture, its hooves making no noise in the deep grass, a dark and powerful shape etched in the moonlight drifting across the field straight to the man.

I knew what I would have to do. I crept along the corral fence, keeping tight to it, until I reached the road. As soon as I was around the corner of the corral with it and the barn between me and the pasture, I started to run as rapidly as I could toward town, my feet plumping softly in the thick dust of the road. I walked this every school day and it had never seemed long before. Now the distance stretched ahead, lengthening in my mind as if to mock me.

I could not let him see me. I kept looking back over my shoulder as I ran. When I saw him swinging into the road, I was well past Johnson's, almost past Shipstead's, striking into the last open stretch to the edge of town. I scurried to the side of the road and behind a clump of bullberry bushes. Panting to get my breath, I crouched there and waited for him to pass. The hoofbeats swelled in my ears, mingled with the pounding beat of my own blood. In my imagination he was galloping furiously and I was positive he was already rushing past me. But when I parted the bushes and pushed forward to peer out, he was moving at a moderate pace and was only almost abreast of me.

He was tall and terrible there in the road, looming up gigantic in the mystic half-light. He was the man I saw that first day, a stranger, dark and forbidding, forging his lone way out of an unknown past in the utter loneliness of his own immovable and instinctive defiance. He was the symbol of all the dim, formless imaginings of danger and terror in the untested realm of human potentialities beyond my understanding. The impact of the menace that marked him was like a physical blow.

I could not help it. I cried out and stumbled and fell. He was off his horse and over me before I could right myself, picking me up, his grasp strong and reassuring. I looked at him, tearful and afraid, and the fear faded from me. He was

46

no stranger. That was some trick of the shadows. He was Shane. He was shaking me gently and smiling at me.

"Bobby boy, this is no time for you to be out. Skip along home and help your mother. I told you everything would be all right."

He let go of me and turned slowly, gazing out across the far sweep of the valley silvered in the moon's glow. "Look at it, Bob. Hold it in your mind like this. It's a lovely land, Bob. A good place to be a boy and grow straight inside as a man should."

My gaze followed his, and I saw our valley as though for the first time and the emotion in me was more than I could stand. I choked and reached out for him and he was not there.

He was rising into the saddle and the two shapes, the man and the horse, became one and moved down the road toward the yellow squares that were the patches of light from the windows of Grafton's building a quarter of a mile away. I wavered a moment, but the call was too strong. I started after him, running frantic in the middle of the road.

Whether he heard me or not, he kept right on. There were several men on the long porch of the building by the saloon doors. Red Marlin's hair made him easy to spot. They were scanning the road intently. As Shane hit the panel of light from the near big front window, the store window, they stiffened to attention. Red Marlin, a startled expression on his face, dived quickly through the doors.

Shane stopped, not by the rail but by the steps on the store side. When he dismounted, he did not slip the reins over the horse's head as the cowboys always did. He left them looped over the pommel of the saddle and the horse seemed to know what this meant. It stood motionless, close by the steps, head up, waiting, ready for whatever swift need.

Shane went along the porch and halted briefly, fronting the two men still there.

"Where's Fletcher?"

They looked at each other and at Shane. One of them started to speak. "He doesn't want – " Shane's voice stopped him. It slapped at them, low and with an edge that cut right into your mind. "Where's Fletcher?"

One of them jerked a hand toward the doors and then, as they moved to shift out of his way, his voice caught them.

"Get inside. Go clear to the bar before you turn."

They stared at him and stirred uneasily and swung together to push through the doors. As the doors came back, Shane grabbed them, one with each hand, and pulled them out and wide open and he disappeared between them.

Clumsy and tripping in my haste, I scrambled up the steps and into the store. Sam Grafton and Mr Weir were the only persons there and they both hurrying to the entrance to the saloon, so intent that they failed to notice me. They stopped in the opening. I crept behind them to my familiar perch on my box where I could see past them.

The big room was crowded. Almost everyone who could be seen regularly around town was there, everyone but our homestead neighbours. There were many others who were new to me. They were lined up elbow to elbow nearly the entire length of the bar. The tables were full and more men were lounging along the far wall. The big round poker table at the back between the stairway to the little balcony and the door to Grafton's office was littered with glasses and chips. It seemed strange, for all the men standing, that there should be an empty chair at the far curve of the table. Someone must have been in that chair, because chips were at the place and a half-smoked cigar, a wisp of smoke curling up from it, was by them on the table.

Red Marlin was leaning against the back wall, behind the chair. As I looked, he saw the smoke and appeared to start a little. With a careful show of casualness he slid into the chair and picked up the cigar.

A haze of thinning smoke was by the ceiling over them all, floating in involved streamers around the hanging lamps. This was Grafton's saloon in the flush of a banner evening's business. But something was wrong, was missing. The hum of activity, the whirr of voices, that should have risen from the scene, been part of it, was stilled in a hush more impressive than any noise could be. The attention of everyone in the room, like a single sense, was centred on that dark figure just inside the swinging doors, back to them and touching them.

This was the Shane of the adventures I had dreamed for him, cool and competent, facing that room full of men in the simple solitude of his own invincible completeness.

His eyes searched the room. They halted on a man sitting at a small table in the front corner with his hat on low over his forehead. With a thump of surprise I recognised it was Stark Wilson and he was studying Shane with a puzzled look on his face. Shane's eyes swept on, checking off each person. They stopped again on a figure over by the wall and the beginnings of a smile showed in them and he nodded almost imperceptibly. It was Chris, tall and lanky, his arm in a sling, and as he caught the nod he flushed a little and shifted his weight from one foot to the other. Then he straightened his shoulders and over his face came a slow smile, warm and friendly, the smile of a man who knows his own mind at last.

But Shane's eyes were already moving on. They narrowed as they rested on Red Marlin. Then they jumped to Will Atkey trying to make himself small behind the bar.

"Where's Fletcher?"

Will fumbled with the cloth in his hands. "I – I don't know. He was here a while ago." Frightened at the sound of his own voice in the stillness, Will dropped the cloth, started to stoop for it, and checked himself, putting his hands to the inside rim of the bar to hold himself steady.

Shane tilted his head slightly so his eyes could clear his hat brim. He was scanning the balcony across the rear of the room. It was empty and the doors there were closed. He stepped forward, disregarding the men by the bar, and

walked quietly past them the long length of the room. He went through the doorway to Grafton's office and into the semi-darkness beyond.

And still the hush held. Then he was in the office doorway again and his eyes bored toward Red Marlin.

"Where's Fletcher?"

The silence was taut and unendurable. It had to break. The sound was that of Stark Wilson coming to his feet in the far front corner. His voice, lazy and insolent, floated down the room

"Where's Starrett?"

While the words yet seemed to hang in the air, Shane was moving toward the front of the room. But Wilson was moving, too. He was crossing toward the swinging doors and he took his stand just to the left of them, a few feet out from the wall. The position gave him command of the wide aisle running back between the bar and the tables and Shane coming forward in it.

Shane stopped about three-quarters of the way forward, about five yards from Wilson. He cocked his head for one quick sideways glance again at the balcony and then he was looking only at Wilson. He did not like the set-up. Wilson had the front wall and he was left in the open of the room. He understood the fact, assessed it, accepted it.

They faced each other in the aisle and the men along the bar jostled one another in their hurry to get to the opposite side of the room. A reckless arrogance was on Wilson, certain of himself and his control of the situation. He was not one to miss the significance of the slim deadliness that was Shane. But even now, I think, he did not believe that anyone in our valley would deliberately stand up to him.

"Where's Starrett?" he said once more, still mocking Shane but making it this time a real question.

The words went past Shane as if they had not been spoken. "I had a few things to say to Fletcher," he said gently. "That can wait. You're a pushing man, Wilson, so I reckon I had better accommodate you."

Wilson's face sobered and his eyes glinted coldly. "I've no quarrel with you," he said flatly, "even if you are Starrett's man. Walk out of here without any fuss and I'll let you go. It's Starrett I want."

"What you want, Wilson, and what you'll get are two different things. Your killing days are done."

Wilson had it now. You could see him grasp the meaning. This quiet man was pushing him just as he had pushed Ernie Wright. As he measured Shane, it was not to his liking. Something that was not fear but a kind of wondering and baffled reluctance showed in his face. And then there was no escape, for that gentle voice was pegging him to the immediate and implacable moment.

"I'm waiting, Wilson. Do I have to crowd you into slapping leather?"

Time stopped and there was nothing in all the world but two men looking into eternity in each other's eyes. And the room rocked in the sudden blur of action indistinct in its incredible swiftness and the roar of their guns was a single sustained blast. And Shane stood, solid on his feet as a rooted oak, and Wilson swayed, his right arm hanging useless, blood beginning to show in a small stream from under the sleeve over the hand, the gun slipping from the numbing fingers.

He backed against the wall, a bitter disbelief twisting his features. His left arm hooked and the second gun was showing and Shane's bullet smashed into his chest and his knees buckled, sliding him slowly down the wall till the lifeless weight of the body toppled it sideways to the floor.

Shane gazed across the space between and he seemed to have forgotten all else as he let his gun ease into the holster. "I gave him his chance," he murmured out of the depths of a great sadness. But the words had no meaning for me, because I noticed on the dark brown of his shirt, low and just above the belt to one side of the buckle, the darker spot gradually widening. Then others noticed, too, and there was a stir in the air and the room was coming to life.

Voices were starting, but no one focused on them. They were snapped short by the roar of a shot from the rear of the room. A wind seemed to whip Shane's shirt at the shoulder and the glass of the front window beyond shattered near the bottom.

Then I saw it.

It was mine alone. The others were turning to stare at the back of the room. My eyes were fixed on Shane and I saw it. I saw the whole man move, all of him, in the single flashing instant. I saw the head lead and the body swing and the driving power of the legs beneath. I saw the arm leap and the hand take the gun in the lightning sweep. I saw the barrel line up – like a finger pointing – and the flame spurt even as the man himself was still in motion.

And there on the balcony Fletcher, impaled in the act of aiming for a second shot, rocked on his heels and fell back into the open doorway behind him. He clawed at the jambs and pulled himself forward. He staggered to the rail and tried to raise the gun. But the strength was draining out of him and he collapsed over the rail, jarring it loose and falling with it.

Across the stunned and barren silence of the room Shane's voice seemed to come from a great distance. "I expect that finishes it," he said. Unconsciously, without looking down, he broke out the cylinder of his gun and reloaded it. The stain on his shirt was bigger now, spreading fanlike above the belt, but he did not appear to know or care. Only his movements were slow, retarded by an unutterable weariness. The hands were sure and steady, but they moved slowly and the gun dropped into the holster of its own weight.

He backed with dragging steps toward the swinging doors until his shoulders touched them. The light in his eyes was unsteady like the flickering of a candle guttering toward darkness. And then, as he stood there, a strange thing happened.

How could one describe it, the change that came over him? Out of the mysterious resources of his will the vitality came. It came creeping, a tide of strength that crept through him and fought and shook off the weakness. It shone in his eyes and they were alive again and alert. It welled up in him, sending that familiar power surging through him again until it was singing again in every vibrant line of him.

He faced that room full of men and read them all with the one sweeping glance and spoke to them in that gentle voice with that quiet, inflexible quality.

"I'll be riding on now. And there's not a one of you that will follow."

He turned his back on them in the indifference of absolute knowledge they would do as he said. Straight and superb, he was silhouetted against the doors and the patch of night above them. The next moment they were closing with a soft swish of sound.

The room was crowded with action now. Men were clustering around the bodies of Wilson and Fletcher, pressing to the bar, talking excitedly. Not a one of them, though, approached too close to the doors. There was a cleared space by the doorway as if someone had drawn a line marking it off.

I did not care what they were doing, or what they were saying. I had to get to Shane. I had to get to him in time. I had to know, and he was the only one who could ever tell me.

I dashed out the store door and I was in time. He was on his horse, already starting away from the steps.

"Shane," I whispered desperately, loud as I dared without the men inside hearing me. "Oh, Shane!"

He heard me and reined around and I hurried to him, standing by a stirrup and looking up.

"Bobby! Bobby boy! What are you doing here?"

"I've been here all along," I blurted out. "You've got to tell me. Was that Wilson – "

He knew what was troubling me. He always knew. "Wilson," he said, "was mighty fast. As fast as I've ever seen."

"I don't care," I said, the tears starting. "I don't care if he was the fastest that ever was. He'd never have been able to shoot you, would he? You'd have got him straight, wouldn't you – if you had been in practice?"

He hesitated a moment. He gazed down at me and into me and he knew. He knew what goes on in a boy's mind and what can help him stay clean inside through the muddled, dirtied years of growing up.

"Sure. Sure, Bob. He'd never even have cleared the holster."

He started to bend down toward me, his hand reaching for my head. But the pain struck him like a whiplash and the hand jumped to his shirt front by the belt, pressing hard, and he reeled a little in the saddle.

The ache in me was more than I could bear. I stared dumbly at him, and because I was just a boy and helpless I turned away and hid my face against the firm, warm flank of the horse.

"Bob."

"Yes, Shane."

"A man is what he is, Bob, and there's no breaking the mould. I tried that and I've lost. But I reckon it was in the cards from the moment I saw a freckled kid on a rail up the road there and a real man behind him, the kind that could back him for the chance another kid never had."

"But – but, Shane, you – "

"There's no going back from a killing, Bob. Right or wrong, the brand sticks and there's no going back. It's up to you now. Go home to your mother and father. Grow strong and straight and take care of them. Both of them."

"Yes, Shane."

"There's only one thing more I can do for them now."

I felt the horse move away from me. Shane was looking down the road and on to the open plain and the horse was obeying the silent command of the reins. He was riding away and I knew that no word or thought could hold him. The big horse, patient and powerful, was already settling into the steady pace that had brought him into our valley, and the two, the man and the horse, were a single dark shape in the road as they passed beyond the reach of the light from the windows.

I strained my eyes after him, and then in the moonlight I could make out the inalienable outline of his figure receding into the distance. Lost in my loneliness, I watched him go, out of town, far down the road where it curved out to the level country beyond the valley. There were men on the porch behind me, but I was aware only of that dark shape growing small and indistinct along the far reach of the road. A cloud passed over the moon and he merged into the general shadow and I could not see him and the cloud passed on and the road was a plain thin ribbon to the horizon and he was gone.

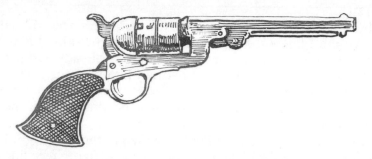

PONY EXPRESS

ROBIN MAY

The truth about the most adventurous job ever offered to teenagers.

"WANTED – young, skinny, wiry fellows, not over 18. Must be expert riders, willing to risk death daily. Orphans preferred. Wages $25 a week . . ."

There has never been a more thrilling passport to danger and adventure than that advertisement, which appeared in a San Francisco paper in 1860. The result – for the lucky few chosen – was a giant relay race with death as the prize for the loser. It was called the Pony Express and it was crazy, heroic, vastly expensive to run, and out-of-date a year after it had started!

Yet the epic of the Pony Express and its young riders, who carried the mails through mountain passes, over deserts and across dangerous Indian country, caught the imagination of the world. It still does more than a century after the very first rider galloped westwards from St Joseph, Missouri, as fast as his horse could carry him one April day in 1860.

Just twelve years before, gold had been found in California, setting off the greatest of all gold rushes. In the booming, gold-rich 1850s the Californians badly needed a first-rate mail service, for they were cut off by more than 3000 kilometres from what was then the rest of the United States to the east. In between was a vast area, not yet fully explored, inhabited by a handful of traders and soldiers and an unknown number of Indians.

Mail was transported by stagecoach, and most of the stages were overloaded and travelled comparatively slowly. As late as 1857, when a 'stagecoach king' named John Butterfield started his Overland Mail, the southern route that he used took twenty-two days to reach California at the very least.

Yet there were many far-sighted Californians who thought that a more central route was not only needed but perfectly possible, and some Western politicians talked a transportation firm, Russell, Majors and Waddell, into setting up a Pony Express.

The three partners feared – rightly as it turned out – that they would lose a fortune, but they worked like slaves to set up a unique mail service. Along the route at regular intervals they built no less than 190 stations. They bought five hundred fast, wiry Indian ponies and hired eighty daring youths.

Their plan was simple but effective. Seventy-five ponies were to be used in each direction for a run, and at every relay station the rider would have just two minutes to hurl his saddle-bags on to a fresh mount before racing off again.

After riding a set distance, one rider would hand over the mail to the next, and so it would continue until journey's end. It was decided that the service would be weekly, but later it was to become twice weekly.

The planned route followed the regular stage line to Salt Lake City, then plunged into a desert region. It ended at Sacramento, the capital of California, after which the mails were transferred to a fast boat, which sped them down to San Francisco on the Pacific coast.

The young riders were not only expected to be young, skinny and wiry, but also utterly fearless and not given to drinking or swearing. They had to swear an oath to that effect:

"I do hereby swear, before the Great and Living God, that during my engagement, and while I am an employee of Russell, Majors & Waddell, I will, under no circumstances, use profane language; that I will drink no intoxicating liquors; that I will not quarrel or fight with any other employee of the firm, and that in every respect I will conduct myself honestly, be faithful to my duties, and so direct all my acts as to win the confidence of my employers. So help me God."

All that and fight Indians too! Yet though a Pony Express rider was given a rifle and a Colt revolver, these were meant to be strictly for self-defence from red men or white. And as well as the weapons, the riders were given a special uniform of red shirt and blue trousers.

Their saddles were lightweight and the mail they carried was confined to telegrams and letters written on thin paper and enclosed in oilcloth to protect them against bad weather.

Incredibly, the three bosses of the enterprise set it up in only sixty days, despite the long distances involved. Then, on 3rd April, 1860, to the cheers of a huge crowd, the first rider set off.

That first run took only ten days and the last rider and pony were given a hero's welcome. When they finished the final stage by boat, the people of San Francisco, no longer isolated from the rest of the nation, gave them a grand parade.

So the Pony Express was in business, and what a business it was! On one incredible run, the teams of riders got through in only six days.

Most of the dauntless young riders survived Indians, wild animals, blizzards, floods and every obstacle in their paths, but one pony reached a Nevada station with its dead rider slumped over the saddle horn, his body riddled with Indian arrows. So tightly was he clutching his horse's mane that it had to be cut from his grasp. But the mail was safe.

The fabulous 'Pony Bob' Haslam was also attacked by Indians, but managed to reach his station after riding 192 kilometres in eight hours, despite having a jaw shattered by an arrow and a bad wound in his left arm. It seemed that nothing but death could deter a Pony Express rider.

The youths were expected to average 14.5 kilometres an

hour whatever happened, but some managed 32. They usually covered from 55 to 120 kilometres depending on the terrain, which varied hugely.

Although, as we have seen, their average age was eighteen, many of the riders were younger. Young Bill Cody, later to become the immortal 'Buffalo Bill', was a mere fourteen when he joined the Pony Express, while 'Bronco Charlie' Miller, who later performed in Buffalo Bill's Wild West Show and lived to be 105, was only eleven! It helped that American boys in the West were almost born in the saddle.

Not only the riders were in peril, for station keepers were also attacked. Newspapers reported many grim items: "The men at Dry Creek Station have all been killed, and it is thought that those at Robert's Creek have met with the same fate."

Sometimes those sent out to support the riders proved less able than the boys at defending themselves. A force of over a hundred men, under a commander who knew nothing of Indian fighting, rode out to punish some Paiutes who were causing the Pony Express trouble, but, in the words of one of the Indians who attacked them: "White men all cry a heap; got no gun, throw 'um away; got no revolver, throw 'um away too; no want to fight any more now; all big scare, just like cattle, run, run, cry, cry, heap cry, same as papoose; no want Injun to kill 'um any more."

He would never have had to say anything as shaming as that about the gallant Pony Express lads!

Human enemies were not the only ones to challenge the riders. Bill Campbell, another youngster who managed to survive to a ripe old age, was riding in the depths of winter when a pack of wolves began chasing him. He heard the howls behind him and, looking round, saw them in full cry and gaining fast, their fangs bared.

He turned round in his saddle, killed two of his pursuers with his Colt, and rode safely away while the rest of the pack stopped to devour their former friends.

The ponies were so fast that Express riders could usually outstrip Indians, who often ran off much-needed horses from the stations.

The riders were not expected to work non-stop, and were allowed occasional rests at the company's expense, when they were housed and fed at their home stations.

Soon not only America but half the world was thrilling to news of the Pony Express. Newspapers in the East depended on the service for up-to-date news and stationed reporters in St Louis, Missouri. From there news was wired which often began with the magical words: "We hear from Pony Express . . ."

Then, just as it must have seemed to everyone that the Pony Express was a colossal success, the need for it vanished overnight and the men who had organised and run it so well were ruined.

The chief reason for the disaster was simple enough – the completion of the transcontinental telegraph, which linked East and West in a way that horse and rider, however courageous, could never do. So the Pony Express collapsed in debt to the tune of thousands of dollars.

These debts were due to the enormous cost of the whole operation, which was far more than could be charged for carrying the mail. When the service ended on 26th October, 1861, 34,753 items of mail had been carried, but, impressive as that figure sounds, the wretched Russell, Majors and Waddell were never able to recover from the sudden closure.

Yet the Pony Express should never be written off as a failure or nothing more than an exciting adventure, for it was a fantastic advertisement for the West at the very moment it was needed. Around 1860, a famous watchword of the nation was 'Go West, young man!' The map of the United States was waiting to be filled in at the centre, and the brave youngsters of the Pony Express had done their spectacular best to help the process along.

Today, one Pony Express station remains as it was in the old days near Hanover, in Kansas, while the original stables of the firm are preserved at St Joseph, Missouri, and contain a thrilling museum. Outside you can see the exact spot from which the first rider set off. But monuments, however exciting, are not needed to keep the story fresh down the years, and the exploits of Bob Haslam, Bronco Charlie Miller, young Bill Cody and the rest of the riders seem more wonderful the more mechanised and streamlined our world becomes.

The galloping hoofs of their ponies are firmly printed on the pages of history and romance, and will not fade as long as the spell of the Old West holds.

THE DOLPHIN CROSSING

JILL PATON WALSH

*In World War Two the British Army has retreated to the shallow beaches
of Dunkirk, and a number of little ships set off from the English coast to
rescue them. Two young boys decide to borrow a boat and help.*

THE COAST OF France started as a thin line of mist on the
horizon. It was mid-morning when it became clear in
the circle of John's binoculars. The country behind the
coastline was flat, for there were no hills to be seen, but there
were a lot of rolling dunes and wide beaches, stretching for
miles. Scanning this alien shore John saw a group of houses
on the beach; the sea-side end of a small town.

They were still following the route of many companion
ships and boats. They had come much farther north than
John had expected, going round the Goodwin sands, and
then striking southeast towards France. John supposed that
the German guns at Calais had closed the more direct route.
Now they were moving in southwards, and a great cloud of
black smoke a few miles to the right must mask the town and
port of Dunkirk.

The sun was shining. The whole scene looked like one of
those great paintings of sea-battles, with modern ships
instead of galleons. All around them, up and down the coast
as far as they could see, there were ships of all sizes. Big naval
ships painted silver-grey were standing offshore, and among

65

them a motley collection of cargo and passenger ships. Beyond them was a stretch of patchy water, blue and indigo, and green in the warm light. And across these wide shallows hundreds of little ships were swarming. There were wrecks too; small boats capsized and drifting, and larger ones grounded and smashed. They sailed through a great patch of floating oil, which stuck to *Dolphin's* paint. And there seemed to be a lot of oil washed up on the beaches; irregular dark shiny patches spreading over the sands to the water's edge. The beach was littered with abandoned lorries and tanks. It all looked very confused.

But it was clear enough what the small boats were doing; they were ferrying to and fro between the shore and the big destroyers and great ships which could not get farther in.

They took *Dolphin* close under the bows of a great destroyer riding at anchor in the sea lanes, and moved towards the shore. Then they saw that the dark patches on the beaches were moving; flowing slowly like spilt water on a flat plate. It wasn't oil; it was great crowds of men. They stood in wide masses on the sands, and the sun struck a dull metallic glint off their steel helmets. Great groups of them moved slowly down towards the water's edge. Long lines of them snaked from behind the dunes, and the head of some of the lines stretched out into the water. They had waded out shoulder deep, and they stood there, quietly, looking all one way – seawards.

John took *Dolphin* in towards one of these lines of men. They could hear the distant noise of guns – a low rumble and now and then a big bang, muffled by distance. But somewhere overhead there was also a droning sound. It got louder and nearer. Looking up, John saw a great swarm of black planes coming from the landward sky. On the beaches men were running for shelter among the dunes, or flinging themselves on their faces in the sand. The planes swooped down, diving low, and flying along the line of the beaches. John saw the black bombs falling in diagonal formation from the swiftly moving planes. A line of fountain-like upward spurts of sand ran along the beach, among the groups of helpless men. From the heart of each jet of sand came a flash of fire, and clouds of thick black smoke. A man with his body stiffly spreadeagled was thrown high in the air, and shot backwards twenty yards from one of them. Then the noise of the explosions crashed round *Dolphin*, wiping all other sounds out entirely, and the beach they were heading for disappeared behind a thick blanket of smoke, which rolled across the water to meet them. A great blast of air smote *Dolphin*, and rocked her violently, and then they were wrapped in blinding, choking smoke.

They coughed and rubbed their eyes. Pat was saying something, but there was only a deafening ringing noise in John's ears. Helplessly he watched Pat's lips moving. The smoke rolled over them and away. They could see to the left now flashes of fire from the muzzles of skyward guns behind the long mole of Dunkirk harbour. A long mole extended seawards on the near side of the harbour, and large ships were tied up there. From the decks of these great ships avenging guns stammered angry retorts into the sky.

On the beaches men were getting to their feet again, and stumbling back into formation. From among them a number of pairs of men were tramping wearily up the beach towards the line of buildings, each pair with a limp body extended between them. The sun broke through the smoke in the misty patches over them.

The planes did not go when they had dropped their bombs. They came back again and again, flying low over the beaches and the shallows, machine-gunning the soldiers and the little boats. A hissing line of bullets spattered the water just in front of *Dolphin*'s prow.

John's hands were clenched on the wheel, but his arms were shaking violently from shoulder to wrist. He could hear his teeth chattering, and a hard lump had grown in his stomach, and was pressing against his ribs, so that he had to force himself to breathe. He stood at the wheel, shaking, and *Dolphin* moved steadily in towards the shore. A smoky haze blurred the whole scene. A choking, bitter smell of burning smarted in John's nostrils at every breath. Pat had gone white, and was crouched down against the bench. His pale eyes looked dark; the pupils were widened with fear. John fixed his eyes on a point on the beach ahead, and tried to steer for it, though he could scarcely make his trembling arms move his clenched fists. A lifeboat, full of soldiers, was just being pushed out into the waves ahead of him. He steered to come in beside it.

The planes were coming back again. The noise of their engines as they plunged low over the sands roared in his ears. He looked, and saw one of them coming straight towards *Dolphin*. He flung himself on the cockpit floor, and at the same moment Pat dropped down beside him, and the wave of noise and the sharp cracking of the plane's machine guns went over and past them. They were still alive. They got up.

Where the lifeboat had been there was a blazing wall of flame on the water. Someone was screaming. The flame floated towards them, and sank. John took the wheel, and brought *Dolphin* on course again. She chugged slowly through charred lumps of floating driftwood, until a gentle scrape on *Dolphin*'s keel told them she had grounded. The tide was low, and a stretch of shallow water still lay between them and the sand. John put the engine out of gear. The two boys stood and looked round. The water was full of floating bodies. They stained the froth on the waves with faintly visible red streaks. They rolled to and fro in the surf. Some of the soldiers waiting in line on the beach had run forward, and were dragging limp wounded figures from the water.

The hard lump in John's stomach suddenly lurched up his throat. He staggered to the side, doubled up, and vomited into the water. As he hung there the body of a man with no face floated by, smelling of charred flesh. He was instantly doubled up again, retching on an empty stomach. Then Pat's hand was on his shoulder, pulling him up.

"Snap out of it, mate. Here's some poor bastards wanting

a lift out of this." Pat's voice came from far away, sounding tight, and unduly loud.

A group of soldiers were wading out towards them, holding their guns over their heads. They came right up to *Dolphin*, and stood waiting waist deep in the sea. Pat took their guns, and John told two of them to hang on to one side, to steady *Dolphin*, while others scrambled over the other side. The water poured from their clothes on to the cockpit floor. They took eight on board, and then John thought they were low enough in the water, and turned the others away. The men who were left pushed *Dolphin* off the sand, grunting under the strain, for she was weighed down now, and turned to scramble through the waves to the beach again.

An agonized expression crossed Pat's face as they went.

"We'll come back for you!" he called to their retreating backs.

"If you don't get sent to the bottom first!" said one of the soldiers beside him.

John was getting used to the different feel of *Dolphin* with her heavy load on board. She was sluggish, and slower to respond to the wheel. Still, when he gave her full power she roared away from the terrible beach towards the tall destroyer waiting off shore.

Over the side of the destroyer hung great swathes of coarse rope netting, draping her wall of riveted plates from stem to stern. Small boats bobbed alongside her all the way, and out of them swarms of soldiers scrambled up the netting, to be pulled over the rails to the decks. John took *Dolphin* up alongside, nosing carefully between two drifters, from whose crowded decks hundreds of climbers were slowly and jerkily heaving themselves away. *Dolphin*'s eight men clambered out of her, making her rock and sway with their movements, and merged with the throng.

Gently John backed *Dolphin* away. When he was clear he gave the wheel to Pat, and looked back at the destroyer through his binoculars. Absurdly, he caught himself trying

to find the men they had just put safely on board, but of course on the thickly crowded decks he could not find them. He picked out somewhere amidships a little board with the name WAKEFUL on it in brass letters. At her bows she carried her code number, painted in huge white letters. John regarded her with satisfaction. She was big, and strong, and armed with her own guns, and the men on board her were going safely home.

As they went back towards the beach, leaving a foaming wake behind them, the attack began again. But this time it was different. John felt oddly numb, almost lightheaded. He saw the exposed position of his own body, sitting in *Dolphin*'s cockpit, as though he were outside himself, seeing the danger from a safe place a little way off. It wasn't really him being fired at; he was somebody else; somebody he didn't really care about much. Pat held the wheel quite steady, and John could hear him in the brief gaps between the deafening noise of exploding shells, cursing volubly in his everyday voice. John listened to the stream of foul language with admiration. He himself knew very few rude words.

The continued shattering noise, the confusion, and this strange feeling of being outside himself, numbed, moving in a daze, blurred John's memories of the hours that followed, so that he could remember them only in patches, and could not have said clearly exactly what they did. They did what all the others were doing; they went in to the beach, picked up a load of men, and took them out to the *Wakeful*. They did it again and again, for hours on end, and John's memory would not sort one journey from another; they were all alike.

He remembered heaving wet bodies over the side into the cockpit. He remembered how they made *Dolphin* take eight men; two on each bunk, two on the cabin floor, two on the benches round the cockpit. Pat kept wanting to pack men in standing up, and so take more, but John was worried about the possibility of capsizing or foundering, if they loaded her too much; as it was she hadn't been built to take eight.

He remembered the roar of the engine, and the swoosh of water as they raced out to the destroyer. Then the grey towering wall of riveted steel, the swinging nets and ladders, the dipping and rocking of *Dolphin* as tired men dragged themselves clumsily out of her and up the side of their homeward-bound ship. And then they went back for more.

Sometimes they went in sunlight, sometimes in black smoke. There were hundreds of other boats bustling along, loaded with men, standing so thick on their decks that they couldn't move without pushing one of their number into the water. The buzzing planes overhead did their best to thin them out. John remembered seeing men falling from the decks of a drifter which was getting peppered with bullets. He felt a wave of anger against the German pilots who shot down such helpless victims. Then he realized that our own pilots would do the same, if the positions of the two armies were reversed. And it struck him suddenly that it was this sort of thing which Andrew had refused to do. For the first time a glimmer of understanding of Andrew's ideas entered his head. But he had no time to think about it. The next second a crackle, a smacking splintering noise of *Dolphin*'s timbers sent him scrambling forward. There was no bad damage done, but a line of holes disfigured the foredeck. Pat made an obscene gesture at the sky. He looked extremely cheerful and quite unafraid. *There is at least as much courage in his bucket*, John thought, *as in mine. More probably.*

Although it was for the sake of all those soldiers that they were there at all, John remembered least of all about the boatloads of men. They were all tired, and wet and cold. Tired most of all. Not the tiredness which makes one sleepy, but a terrible weariness of body and mind, which made them slow in all their movements, and glazed their eyes, and made their faces blank. Pat was very good at managing them. He called the men "Mate!" and the officers "gaffer!" and he shouted "One more inside!" and "Hold tight!" just like the conductor of a London bus. He raised grins on tired faces, and nobody seemed to mind doing what he told them.

Of course, some of the passengers caught John's attention, and so he remembered them later. One officer said to him, "I've got a boy about your age," and produced a soaking wet snapshot to show him. It was of a boy in scout's uniform. There was one group who came aboard every one still carrying pack and rifle, unlike most. In charge of them was a very quiet officer, and a very fierce sergeant, with a round baby face, who yelled at them as though he had them on parade. They waded into the water in a line as straight as a ruler, and they were much more cheerful than most. They even sang as *Dolphin* took them across to safety in the *Wakeful*. The song was about the round-faced sergeant. It went to the tune of 'It's a long way to Tipperary'. The words made even Pat raise his eyebrows.

Towards evening, in one of Pat's spells at the wheel John poured some of Crossman's soup into mugs for supper. They drank soup and ate biscuits without stopping; one hand was enough to steady *Dolphin's* wheel. They had got used to noise, and the gunshot, and the blast from bombs and shells. They didn't jump any more, they just carried on. But the evening seemed long. They were very tired now. But at last dusk crept upon them.

And with the dusk, slowly, so that they hardly noticed it at first, the fighting died down. No more planes came over, the guns on shore fired only sporadically, and there was a lull. They went back to the beach in the unaccustomed quiet, straining their eyes in the half-light. A small motor-cruiser which had worked beside them all day was going in the same direction a little way off on the port side. Looking towards her John saw a dark round shadow bobbing in the water in front of her. The next instant she had struck it.

The explosion stunned John. He struggled to see and hear, to realize what had happened. A great wave had

washed over *Dolphin*, and he was standing in a few inches of water.

"Pat!" he called. "Pat, where are you?"

"Here," said a voice at his feet. Pat had been knocked over by the blast. He scrambled up again, and they looked for the little cruiser. There was not the smallest trace of her. Pat was looking at John in alarm. And John realized that there was a nasty hot, wet feeling in his left arm. He looked down at it, and saw that he was pouring with blood. He felt weak and faint.

Pat did not panic. He got John lying on a bunk, and pulled his arm out of the sleeve of his sweater. He opened the first-aid box Crossman had given them. There was a ragged piece of metal stuck in John's upper arm. It was bleeding profusely. Somehow Pat got the thing out. John was looking the other way, biting his lip. It didn't hurt as much as he feared; it was still numb, but the iodine Pat used to clean it up with hurt so much he could hardly stop himself crying out. Pat put a lot of bandage round his arm, and then got the brandy bottle, and insisted that John drank some.

"I'll be all right now," said John, getting to his feet. "Thank goodness it was my left arm, and not my right." As he spoke they heard shouting, coming from just outside. *Dolphin* had been drifting, and had nearly run aground on the beach. And a mob of soldiers were scrambling out towards her, shouting. "A boat! A boat!"

John grabbed the wheel, and swung it hard round. The prow turned away from the beach, bringing her sideways on the shore. A stab of pain from his shoulder stopped John's hand halfway to the switch to put the engine on. A dozen hands grabbed *Dolphin*. She tilted down towards them. A rabble of hysterical men were all trying to board her at once.

"Let go!" cried John. "You'll capsize her!" Pat grabbed a saucepan from the galley, and laid about him like a fishwife, smashing at the knuckles of the raiders, banging them till they let go. Cries and curses rang through the growing darkness.

Suddenly a voice from the shore cried, "Let go that boat!" A man waded out towards them. He was only a private, but he still had his gun. One of the mob had succeeded in getting aboard. The newcomer looked at him.

"You're an officer, aren't you? Where are your men?" There was no answer. Then, very slowly, the officer got over the side, and let himself down into the water. He waded away towards the beach.

"Right. One at a time now." The private got them aboard at gun point. "Had a rough time, this lot," he observed to Pat, as though talking about the weather. But now they were aboard they seemed just like the rest; tired, silent, wet, with that expression half-way between blankness and patience on their faces.

John put *Dolphin* full speed ahead, and made for *Wakeful* again.

"You all right?" asked Pat anxiously.

"Fine," said John. But his arm hurt, and he let Pat take the wheel. Pat managed it well, even the tricky manoeuvre edging up to the side of the destroyer.

"Don't take long to learn to drive these things," he observed.

John grinned. "Wait till you meet some real weather!" he said.

When they reached *Wakeful*, her officers were leaning over the rail. "Last few now," they were calling down. "We can't take any more. We'll be back tomorrow, God willing!"

Pat helped their passengers on to the ladders. Looking up to see them go, John saw stars pricking the wide black sky. His legs felt soft and bendy. He sat down. Under his instructions Pat took *Dolphin* out half a mile, to the sand-bar which bounded the sea-road along the shore. Here the water was shallow, and they let out the sea anchor among a group of drifters and tugs, whose crews were also taking a brief rest, under cover of the welcome night.

They drank some more of Crossman's soup, and ate plenty of the funny coarse biscuit with guava jam. It all tasted very odd, but it was filling. Then they lay down on the bunks to get some sleep. The bedding was soaking wet from having been sat on by all those wet soldiers, but John was too exhausted to care. He was asleep almost as soon as he lay down.

*   *   *

John dreamed that they were surrounded by frantic men trying to climb on board; one of them had him by the arm, and was dragging at him, trying to pull himself up. The boat seemed already to be full of water; he felt wet and cold. Then he opened his eyes. Above him was the roof strut of *Dolphin*'s cabin. He felt himself floating gently. *Dolphin* was almost still, quietly riding on tranquil water, but the slight, smooth movements of her hull gave him the sensation of floating. The water he felt must be in the cabin. He woke abruptly, and sat up. She was sinking!

He looked at the dry floor boards of the cabin for several seconds before he realized that it was only the bedding in the bunk he lay in which was wet. The damp had soaked through his own clothes to his skin, and he was shivering in his clammy garb.

He got out of the bunk. But the sense of danger had not left him; hadn't there been boarders? No; the dragging at his arm was only the tightness of the bandages on the sore wound. The noise of the scrabbling, grasping hands was only a light scratching tapping noise on the side of the hull. Suddenly he remembered the mine which had blown up the motor boat yesterday. His heart was pounding and his tongue had gone dry. He went to look what it was.

A thin grey light filtered through the cabin door. Outside, it was light, but a white mist hung over the sea, shutting everything out of sight. None of the ships that had been anchored around them the night before was visible. The noise on the side of the boat was made by a drowned man, washing gently against her. He floated face upwards, and the water lapped into his staring eyes. John felt a surge of relief, but the glint in the man's eyes made him turn away shuddering. He fended him off with the boat hook.

Back in the cabin Pat was still sleeping soundly. John opened the flask of coffee Crossman had given them. What remained in it was cold and horrid. He slopped it out of the porthole, and put a kettle on the stove. There was a small locker in the galley, where food was kept when the family took *Dolphin* sailing. John found three old, battered teabags, and some lump sugar lying in it. He made tea in a big saucepan, refilled the flask and poured two cups from the pan. He worked clumsily, using only one hand; his hurt arm was now very stiff. And the quietness quickly got on his nerves, so that he was glad when the tea was made, and he had an excuse to wake Pat.

"Did you hear that bang in the night?" Pat asked as they drank tea, and chewed more biscuit.

"What bang?"

"Cor, if you had heard it, you wouldn't need to ask. One helluva bang, there was. You must have been out like a light; it would have woken you otherwise."

"A big bomb, I suppose."

"Came from out at sea somewhere."

"Oh." John couldn't summon much interest in it.

"You reckon we ought to scarper off home?" asked Pat.

"No, not yet. Unless you've had enough, Pat. I wouldn't blame you. Don't be afraid to say."

"Not me. And there are a hell of a lot of soldiers still on that beach. I'd bet *they've* had enough. I was thinking of your arm, mate."

"I'm OK. But you'll have to manage the boat most of the time. I don't think I can handle the wheel much. My arm's very stiff this morning."

"That's all right. I can steer your boat easy enough."

"If we have another calm day . . ." thought John to himself.

There was still nothing but mist outside. They had to use the compass to work out which way to head for the beach, although when they looked up they could see a pale blue sky with some clouds in it. The mist was only a few yards thick; only a haze on the surface of the water.

"It's good cover, anyway," said Pat.

It muffled sound as well as sight. They were quite near in before they heard the gunfire rolling from the hinterland behind the beaches. But they had not heard it for many minutes before they knew that it was nearer than it had been yesterday; the rearguard had given a few miles. It proved impossible to work as they had done yesterday, because there were no big ships there to take on men. With Pat at the wheel *Dolphin* nosed up and down the coastline a mile or so both ways, but there was no doubt about it; there were no big ships about.

"They've all gone off home, and haven't got back yet," said Pat. "What do we do now, skipper?"

"We could hang around for a bit, and see if one turns up. I suppose it would be worth waiting till noon; but we have to start back early in the afternoon; we mustn't risk running out of petrol in mid-Channel."

Hanging around wasn't much fun. They couldn't see far in the wreathing sea-mist, and they decided to save petrol by switching the engine off, and just letting her drift gently. Pat smoked a lot of the cigarettes Crossman had given them. John just sat. It was very nasty, being so close to danger, and having nothing to do to take one's mind off it. But they didn't have to wait till noon; long before then a filthy battered coal-carrying tramp ship arrived in the sea lanes; and appearing miraculously out of the dissolving mist, a handful of little boats began to ply between her and the shore.

John turned on *Dolphin*'s engine, and Pat took her towards the beach at random. They were both immensely relieved to be able to get to work again. The mist had dissolved into hazy sunlight, and the noise of battle was growing.

They found a change in the beach. The men had built themselves a makeshift pier, by pushing a line of lorries out into the water, and making a footway of planks laid over them. Men were scrambling dryshod over this gangway, and getting into boats drawn up at the end of it. A lifeboat and a small trawler were loading up, tied to either side of the last lorry, which was so deep that the waves washed over its roof. *Dolphin* joined them. It was much easier getting men aboard from the makeshift jetty than it had been yesterday; but it was harder getting them onto the ship. The tramp ship had no nets, only ladders, up which men had to climb in single file, painfully slowly. Pat became nearly frantic with impatience while they waited for their turn under the ladder, and then waited for their men to climb out one by one.

"Steady on, Pat," said John to him at last. "We are doing as well as we can. Best not to fret about it."

"We could get another whole boatload out here in the time it's taking us to get them on to that bloody ladder!"

"We won't do any better if we get worked up about it."

"At last!" said Pat, swinging *Dolphin* away as soon as the last man got one foot on the first rung of the ladder.

"Watch it, mate!" said John protesting. "You nearly gave him a ducking."

"We're in a hurry!"

"Don't be a fool, Pat. We aren't in a hurry. We just take it steadily, and keep calm."

Pat flushed. "Oh, yea. It doesn't matter how many we leave on them flaming beaches. We just keep calm!"

"I don't know what makes you think it matters less to me than to you." Anger made John's voice stiff and cold.

"The way you went on about them. 'England needs soldiers' you said. 'Save our army so they can fight again.' Just push them around the country like they was toys on your map. I don't give a damn whether they can fight again; I just want to get them out of here! One of the poor bastards what has to get left behind might be my dad!"

John's anger disappeared at once. He waited a long time before answering. "Well, can you think of anything we can do to work faster?" he asked.

"No, blast it, I can't," said Pat. He grinned at John. His anger too had blown over.

Dolphin pulled up again at the jetty. But before anyone got on board an officer appeared, and hailed them. He was carrying despatches, and he wanted a fast boat to take him north, and land him on some beach there, quickly.

"We'll be moving into heavy fire. You're free to refuse," he said curtly.

"'Op in, codger," returned Pat disrespectfully.

"As fast as she'll go, please," said the officer, getting in.

"My turn at the wheel now, Pat," said John, slightly alarmed at the thought of Pat's inexperienced hand taking *Dolphin* at full speed. He found he could use his stiff arm if he really tried. Dolphin sprang away, cutting a path between two walls of foam. The officer was looking from one to another of them.

"In the name of heaven, how old are you?" he asked.

"Old enough to handle a boat, sir," said John.

"You'd better put me down at once, and get home," said the officer angrily. "This isn't a playground!"

"Thought you was in a hurry," said Pat. The officer looked at them again. Their faces were streaked with

black from the smoke; the set of their mouths, had they but known it, showed the tiredness, and the strain.

"How long have you been here?" he asked in a changed tone of voice.

"Since yesterday morning, sir," said John. Overhead they heard the droning noise of oncoming planes.

"Don't look up; they won't be ours," said the officer with bitterness in his voice. "Not a single one of our blasted air force to stop them murdering us." Then in his normal tone. "Nearly at La Panne now. Can you get close inshore and put me off?"

The beaches here were being heavily shelled from the shore. It was the same bedlam of smoke and noise that yesterday had been. But the protecting numbness had worn off. John was very frightened again, and Pat too was jumpy. They took the officer in to shallow water. Just before he jumped over the side he said. "Enough's enough. You've done your bit, and more. Get home now. I hope you make it." Then he was gone, wading towards the terrible inferno on the beach.

"He's right," said John, looking at his watch. "We'll have to get back now, if we're to be sure our petrol will see us safely home."

"You mean just quit, now?"

"Well, we aren't going home empty. Take her back to that crummy jetty, and we'll pick up a load of men to take with us." John had had as much as he could take of managing the wheel; he gave it back to Pat. They went back to Bray, where the crazy little jetty of half submerged lorries was still crowded with men. The coal ship however had gone, and the horizon was empty.

On the end lorry someone was directing the line of men. They came up in order, and scrambled down into *Dolphin*. Pat held the wheel steady, and John, with his good arm, took such packs and rifles as the men still had, and told them where to sit. A little way down the line there was some pushing and scuffling.

"Right. That's all now," said John.

"Another bus along in a minute!" called Pat. A faint grin appeared on some of the weary faces in the row. Then the pushing arrived at the top of the line. It was caused by two men carrying an officer on a stretcher.

"Can you take him?" they asked John.

"I'm sorry, no," said John firmly. "We're full up."

The stretcher bearers were tired. They looked around at the dark sea.

"He should be in hospital," one of them said. A great silence had fallen over the waiting line of men. Nobody moved, nobody spoke. The man directing operations looked down at the water, as though it were no affair of his.

Then suddenly the man on the stretcher groaned. He stiffened, and tossed his head.

"Right, bring him down," said Pat. "We'll fit him in somehow."

"I'm sorry, Pat, but we can't," said John.

"Oh, have a heart, mate! We can tie the stretcher on the cabin roof or something. But we can't just leave him to rot!"

"We can't take him. We can't possibly. *Dolphin*'s too far down in the water as it is. We can't risk making her any heavier."

"One can't make much difference," said Pat. His mouth was set in a stubborn line. "If it's a risk, let's take it. We taken plenty already."

"I'm sorry . . . but no. We have eight men on board, and ourselves. We can't risk ten lives for one. It isn't fair to ask it."

"It's a risk we got to take. You ain't really saying you can look at that poor devil and say we're going to leave him? Ain't you human?"

"*You're* a flaming idiot!" cried John in exasperation. "This boat won't take any more, and that's that!"

"We've carried him for three days," said a voice from the jetty. "The morphia has worn off. He needs a doctor."

"I don't see why we can't put him on top of the cabin," said Pat sullenly.

John struggled to master his rising anger. "Look, you've only been in a boat for a few hours, Pat, and it's been the calmest day for years. If a bit of wind gets up we'll be shipping water, and in bad trouble. We are chancing a lot on the hope that there won't be a swell in the Channel as it is . . ."

"It would be all right, then, if I got out?" said one of the soldiers from behind him. John turned to look at him. He was a lanky young man, with a cut on one cheek. He looked tired, and the empty expression on his face was unchanged as he spoke. John nodded.

"Rightie-ho. I'm off then," said the soldier, scrambling up the side of the nearest lorry. Several hands were extended to help him up, and to pat him on the back when he got there. Nobody said anything.

The stretcher was lowered down towards them. The man on it screamed when it hit the deck with a jerk. With a little difficulty they made room for the stretcher in the cabin, on one of the bunks. Then at last Pat took *Dolphin* chugging away from the jetty, and roaring across the bay. John was full of admiration for the unknown soldier who had given up his place, full of concern for him. *"I hope another boat comes for him soon"* he thought.

But when they were speeding up the sea-lane to the north, well out to sea, out of range of the guns at La Panne, and the sun shone through the grey afternoon, a great surge of relief and joy lifted John's heart. They had done it; and what was more, it was over. They would be home in a couple of hours; they were out of gunrange already. The thought of home, with real food, and safety, and hearing things on the wireless instead of living through them seemed like heaven on earth.

THROUGH THE TUNNEL

DORIS LESSING

GOING TO THE shore on the first morning of the holiday, the young English boy stopped at a turning of the path and looked down at a wild and rocky bay, and then over to the crowded beach he knew so well from other years. His mother walked on in front of him, carrying a bright striped bag in one hand. Her other arm, swinging loose, was very white in the sun. The boy watched that white, naked arm, and turned his eyes, which had a frown behind them, towards the bay and back again to his mother. When she felt he was not with her, she swung around. "Oh there you are, Jerry!" she said. She looked impatient, then smiled. "Why, darling, would you rather not come with me? Would you rather –" She frowned, conscientiously worrying over what amusements he might secretly be longing for which she had been too busy or too careless to imagine. He was very familiar with that anxious, apologetic smile. Contrition sent him running after her. And yet, as he ran, he looked back over his shoulder at the wild bay; and all morning, as he played on the safe beach, he was thinking of it.

Next morning, when it was time for the routine of swimming and sunbathing, his mother said, "Are you tired of the usual beach, Jerry? Would you like to go somewhere else?"

"Oh, no!" he said quickly, smiling at her out of that unfailing impulse of contrition – a sort of chivalry. Yet, walking down the path with her, he blurted out, "I'd like to go and have a look at those rocks down there."

She gave the idea her attention. It was a wild-looking place, and there was no one there, but she said, "Of course, Jerry. When you've had enough, come to the big beach. Or just go straight back to the villa, if you like." She walked away, that bare arm, now slightly reddened from yesterday's sun, swinging. And he almost ran after her again, feeling it unbearable that she should go by herself, but he did not.

She was thinking, Of course he's old enough to be safe without me. Have I been keeping him too close? He mustn't feel he ought to be with me. I must be careful.

He was an only child, eleven years old. She was a widow. She was determined to be neither possessive nor lacking in devotion. She went worrying off to her beach.

As for Jerry, once he saw that his mother had gained her beach, he began the steep descent to the bay. From where he was, high up among red-brown rocks, it was a scoop of moving bluish green fringed with white. As he went lower, he saw that it spread among small promontories and inlets of rough, sharp rock, and the crisping, lapping surface showed stains of purple and darker blue. Finally, as he ran sliding and scraping down the last few yards, he saw an edge of white surf, and the shallow, luminous movement of water over white sand, and, beyond that, a solid, heavy blue.

He ran straight into the water and began swimming. He was a good swimmer. He went out fast over the gleaming sand, over a middle region where rocks lay like discoloured monsters under the surface, and then he was in the real sea – a warm sea where irregular cold currents from the deep water shocked his limbs.

When he was so far out that he could look back not only on the little bay but past the promontory that was between it and the big beach, he floated on the buoyant surface and looked for his mother. There she was, a speck of yellow under an umbrella that looked like a slice of orange peel. He swam back to shore, relieved at being sure she was there, but all at once very lonely.

On the edge of a small cape that marked the side of the bay away from the promontory was a loose scatter of rocks. Above them, some boys were stripping off their clothes. They came running, naked, down to the rocks. The English boy swam towards them, and kept his distance at a stone's throw. They were of that coast, all of them burned smooth dark brown, and speaking a language he did not understand. To be with them, of them, was a craving that filled his whole body. He swam a little closer; they turned and watched him with narrowed, alert dark eyes. Then one smiled and waved. It was enough. In a minute, he had swum in and was on the rocks beside them, smiling with a desperate, nervous supplication. They shouted cheerful greetings at him, and then, as he preserved his nervous, uncomprehending smile, they understood that he was a foreigner strayed from his own beach, and they proceeded to forget him. But he was happy. He was with them.

They began diving again and again from a high point into a well of blue sea between rough, pointed rocks. After they had dived and come up, they swam around, hauled themselves up, and waited their turn to dive again. They were big boys – men to Jerry. He dived, and they watched him, and when he swam around to take his place, they made way for him. He felt he was accepted, and he dived again, carefully, proud of himself.

Soon the biggest of the boys poised himself, shot down into the water, and did not come up. The others stood about, watching. Jerry, after waiting for the sleek brown head to appear, let out a yell of warning; they looked at him idly and turned their eyes back towards the water. After a long time, the boy came up on the other side of a big dark rock, letting the air out of his lungs in a sputtering gasp and a shout of triumph. Immediately, the rest of them dived in. One moment, the morning seemed full of chattering boys; the next, the air and the surface of the water were empty. But through the heavy blue, dark shapes could be seen moving and groping.

Jerry dived, shot past the school of underwater swimmers, saw a black wall of rock looming at him, touched it, and bobbed up at once to the surface, where the wall was a low barrier he could see across. There was no one visible; under him, in the water, the dim shapes of the swimmers had disappeared. Then one, and then another of the boys came up on the far side of the barrier of rock, and he understood that they had swum through some gap or hole in it. He plunged down again. He could see nothing through the stinging salt water but the blank rock. When he came up, the boys were all on the diving rock, preparing to attempt the feat again. And now, in a panic of failure, he yelled up, in English, "Look at me! Look!" and he began splashing and kicking in the water like a foolish dog.

They looked down gravely, frowning. He knew the frown. At moments of failure, when he clowned to claim his mother's attention, it was with just this grave, embarrassed inspection that she rewarded him. Through his hot shame, feeling the pleading grin on his face like a scar that he could never remove, he looked up at the group of big brown boys on the rock and shouted, "*Bonjour! Merci! Au revoir! Monsieur, monsieur!*" while he hooked his fingers round his ears and waggled them.

Water surged into his mouth; he choked, sank, came up. The rock, lately weighed with boys, seemed to rear up out of the water as their weight was removed. They were flying down past him, now, into the water; the air was full of falling bodies. Then the rock was empty in the hot sunlight. He counted one, two, three . . .

At fifty, he was terrified. They must all be drowning beneath him, in the water caves of the rock! At a hundred, he stared around him at the empty hillside, wondering if he should yell for help. He counted faster, faster, to hurry them up, to bring them to the surface quickly, to drown them quickly – anything rather than the terror of counting on and on into the blue emptiness of the morning. And then, at a hundred and sixty, the water beyond the rock was full of boys blowing like brown whales. They swam back to the shore without a look at him.

He climbed back to the diving rock and sat down, feeling the hot roughness of it under his thighs. The boys were gathering up their bits of clothing and running off along the shore to another promontory. They were leaving to get away from him. He cried openly, fists in his eyes. There was no one to see him, and he cried himself out.

It seemed to him that a long time had passed, and he swam out to where he could see his mother. Yes, she was still there, a yellow spot under an orange umbrella. He swam back to the big rock, climbed up, and dived into the blue pool among the fanged and angry boulders. Down he went, until he touched the wall of rock again. But the salt was so painful in his eyes that he could not see.

He came to the surface, swam to shore and went back to the villa to wait for his mother. Soon she walked slowly up the path, swinging her striped bag, the flushed, naked arm dangling beside her. "I want some swimming goggles," he panted, defiant and beseeching.

She gave him a patient, inquisitive look as she said casually, "Well, of course, darling."

But now, now, now! He must have them this minute, and no other time. He nagged and pestered until she went with him to a shop. As soon as she had bought the goggles, he grabbed them from her hand as if she were going to claim them for herself, and was off, running down the steep path to the bay.

Jerry swam out to the big barrier rock, adjusted the goggles, and dived. The impact of the water broke the rubber-enclosed vacuum, and the goggles came loose. He understood that he must swim down to the base of the rock from the surface of the water. He fixed the goggles tight and firm, filled his lungs, and floated, face down, on the water.

Now he could see. It was as if he had eyes of a different kind –fish-eyes that showed everything clear and delicate and wavering in the bright water.

Under him, six or seven feet down, was a floor of perfectly clean, shining white sand, rippled firm and hard by the tides. Two greyish shapes steered there, like long, rounded pieces of wood or slate. They were fish. He saw them nose towards each other, poise motionless, make a dart forward, swerve off, and come around again. It was like a water dance. A few inches above them the water sparkled as if sequins were dropping through it. Fish again – myriads of minute fish, the length of his fingernail, were drifting through the water, and in a moment he could feel the innumerable tiny touches of them against his limbs. It was like swimming in flaked silver. The great rock the big boys had swum through rose sheer out of the white sand, black, tufted lightly with greenish weed. He could see no gap in it. He swam down to its base.

Again and again he rose, took, a big chestful of air, and went down. Again and again he groped over the surface of the rock, feeling it, almost hugging it in the desperate need to find the entrance. And then, once, while he was clinging to the black wall, his knees came up and he shot his feet out forward and they met no obstacle. He had found the hole.

He gained the surface, clambered about the stones that littered the barrier rock until he found a big one, and, with this in his arms, let himself down over the side of the rock. He dropped, with the weight, straight to the sandy floor. Clinging tight to the anchor of stone, he lay on his side and looked in under the dark shelf at the place where his feet had gone. He could see the hole. It was an irregular, dark gap, but he could not see deep into it. He let go of his anchor, clung with his hands to the edge of the hole, and tried to push himself in.

He got his head in, found his shoulders jammed, moved them in sidewise, and was inside as far as his waist. He could see nothing ahead. Something soft and clammy

touched his mouth, he saw a dark frond moving against the greyish rock, and panic filled him. He thought of octopuses, of clinging weed. He pushed himself backward and caught a glimpse, as he retreated, of a harmless tentacle of seaweed drifting in the mouth of the tunnel. But it was enough. He reached the sunlight, swam to shore, and lay on the diving rock. He looked down into the blue well of water. He knew he must find his way through that cave, or hole, or tunnel, and out the other side.

First, he thought, he must learn to control his breathing. He let himself down into the water with another big stone in his arms, so that he could lie effortlessly on the bottom of the sea. He counted. One, two, three. He counted steadily. He could hear the movement of blood in his chest. Fifty-one, fifty-two . . . His chest was hurting. He let go of the rock and went up into the air. He saw that the sun was low. He rushed to the villa and found his mother at her supper. She said only, "Did you enjoy yourself?" and he said, "Yes."

All night, the boy dreamed of the water-filled cave in the rock, and as soon as breakfast was over he went to the bay.

That night, his nose bled badly. For hours he had been underwater, learning to hold his breath, and now he felt weak and dizzy. His mother said, "I shouldn't overdo things, darling, if I were you."

That day and the next, Jerry exercised his lungs as if everything, the whole of his life, all that he would become, depended upon it. And again his nose bled at night, and his mother insisted on his coming with her the next day. It was a torment to him to waste a day of his careful self-training, but he stayed with her at that other beach, which now seemed a place for small children, a place where his mother might lie safe in the sun. It was not his beach.

He did not ask for permission, on the following day, to go to his beach. He went, before his mother could consider the complicated rights and wrongs of the matter. A day's rest, he discovered had improved his count by ten. The big boys had made the passage while he counted a hundred and sixty. He had been counting fast, in his fright. Probably now, if he tried, he could get through that long tunnel, but he was not going to try yet. A curious, most unchildlike persistence, a controlled impatience, made him wait. In the meantime, he lay underwater on the white sand, littered now by stones he had brought down from the upper air, and studied the entrance to the tunnel. He knew every jut and corner of it, as far as it was possible to see. It was as if he already felt its sharpness about his shoulders.

He sat by the clock in the villa, when his mother was not near, and checked his time. He was incredulous and then proud to find he could hold his breath without strain for two minutes. The words 'two minutes', authorized by the clock, brought the adventure that was so necessary to him close.

In another four days, his mother said casually one morning they must go home. On the day before they left, he would do it. He would do it if it killed him, he said defiantly to himself. But two days before they were to leave – a day of triumph when he increased his count by fifteen – his nose bled so badly that he turned dizzy and had to lie limply over the big rock like a bit of seaweed, watching the thick red blood flow on to the rock and trickle slowly down to the sea. He was frightened. Supposing he turned dizzy in the tunnel? Supposing he died there, trapped? Supposing – his head went around, in the hot sun, and he almost gave up. He thought he would return to the house and lie down, and next summer, perhaps, when he had another year's growth in him – *then* he would go through the hole.

But even after he had made the decision, or thought he had, he found himself sitting up on the rock and looking down into the water, and he knew that now, this moment, when his nose had only just stopped bleeding, when his head was still sore and throbbing – this was the moment when he would try. If he did not do it now, he never would. He was trembling with fear that he would not go, and he was trembling with horror at that long, long tunnel under the rock, under the sea. Even in the open sunlight, the barrier rock seemed very wide and very heavy; tons of rock pressed down on where he would go. If he died there, he would lie until one day – perhaps not before next year – those big boys would swim into it and find it blocked.

He put on his goggles, fitted them tight, tested the vacuum. His hands were shaking. Then he chose the biggest stone he could carry and slipped over the edge of the rock until half of him was in the cool, enclosing water and half in the hot sun. He looked up once at the empty sky, filled his lungs once, twice, and then sank fast to the bottom with the stone. He let it go and began to count. He took the edges of the hole in his hands and drew himself into it, wriggling his shoulders in sidewise as he remembered he must, kicking himself along with his feet.

Soon he was clear inside. He was in a small rock-bound hole filled with yellowish-grey water. The water was pushing him up against the roof. The roof was sharp and pained his back. He pulled himself along with his hands – fast, fast – and used his legs as levers. His head knocked against something; a sharp pain dizzied him. Fifty, fifty-one, fifty-two . . . He was without light, and the water seemed to press upon him with the weight of rock. Seventy-one, seventy-two . . . There was no strain on his lungs. He felt like an inflated balloon, his lungs were so light and easy, but his head was pulsing.

He was being continually pressed against the sharp roof, which felt slimy as well as sharp. Again he thought of octopuses, and wondered if the tunnel might be filled with weed that could tangle him. He gave himself a panicky, convulsive kick forward, ducked his head, and swam. His feet and hands moved freely, as if in open water. The hole must have widened out. He thought he must be swimming fast, and he was frightened of banging his head if the tunnel narrowed.

A hundred, a hundred and one . . . The water paled. Victory filled him. His lungs were beginning to hurt. A few more strokes and he would be out. He was counting wildly; he said a hundred and fifteen, and then, a long time later, a hundred and fifteen again. The water was a clear jewel-green all around him. Then he saw, above his head, a crack running up through the rock. Sunlight was falling through it, showing the clean dark rock of the tunnel, a single mussel shell, and darkness ahead.

He was at the end of what he could do. He looked up at the crack as if it were filled with air and not water, as if he could put his mouth to it to draw in air. A hundred and fifteen, he heard himself say inside his head – but he had said that long ago. He must go on into the blackness

ahead, or he would drown. His head was swelling, his lungs cracking. A hundred and fifteen, a hundred and fifteen pounded through his head, and he feebly clutched at rocks in the dark, pulling himself forward, leaving the brief space of sunlit water behind. He was no longer quite conscious. He struggled on in the darkness between lapses into unconsciousness. An immense, swelling pain filled his head, and then the darkness cracked with an explosion of green light. His hands, groping forward, met nothing, and his feet, kicking back, propelled him out into the open sea.

He drifted to the surface, his face turned up to the air. He was gasping like a fish. He felt he would sink now and drown; he could not swim the few feet back to the rock. Then he was clutching it and pulling himself up on to it. He lay face down, gasping. He could see nothing but a red-veined, clotted dark. His eyes must have burst, he thought, they were full of blood. He tore off his goggles and a gout of blood went into the sea. His nose was bleeding, and the blood had filled the goggles.

He scooped up handfuls of water from the cool, salty sea, to splash on his face, and did not know whether it was blood or salt water he tasted. After a time, his heart quietened, his eyes cleared, and he sat up. He could see the local boys diving and playing half a mile away. He did not want them. He wanted nothing but to get back home and lie down.

In a short while, Jerry swam to shore and climbed slowly up the path to the villa. He flung himself on the bed and slept, waking at the sound of feet on the path outside. His mother was coming back. He rushed to the bathroom, thinking she must not see his face with bloodstains, or tearstains, on it. He came out of the bathroom and met her as she walked into the villa, smiling, her eyes lighting up.

"Have a nice morning?" she asked, laying her hand on his warm brown shoulder a moment.

"Oh, yes, thank you," he said.

"You look a bit pale." And then, sharp and anxious, "How did you bang your head?"

"Oh, just banged it," he told her.

She looked at him closely. He was strained. His eyes were glazed-looking. She was worried. And then she said to herself, Oh, don't fuss! Nothing can happen. He can swim like a fish.

They sat down to lunch together.

"Mummy," he said, "I can stay under water for two minutes – three minutes, at least." It came bursting out of him.

"Can you, darling," she said. "Well, I shouldn't overdo it. I don't think you ought to swim any more today."

She was ready for a battle of wits, but he gave in at once. It was no longer of the least importance to go to the bay.

BOY BLUE
THE CRAB-CATCHER

GEORGE LAMMING

"**L**ET'S GO," Trumper said. He had hardly spoken when the little crabs appeared. They were nearer the sea now. When we had seen them last they had crawled up to the grape vine, but they must have cut a way back through the sand while we were watching the fisherman. Their eyes were raised, and they limped slowly towards the sea. The sand seemed firmer where they were.

"You like crab?" Boy Blue asked. He smiled as he asked the question.

"I like crab," Trumper said, "but these too small." He too smiled as he spoke.

"What don't kill does fatten," Boy Blue said.

Boy Blue left us and crept towards the crabs approaching them from the back. Crab-catching was a pastime which we used to test our speed as well as lightness of touch. After heavy rains the village was often invaded by crabs, large blue-back creatures sprawling stupidly here and there to get their bearings. The men and boys came out in droves with sticks and pokers and traps of every description. Children and women screamed when they saw the catch. Sometimes it yielded hundreds of crabs, and the boys and men who had trapped them made a prosperous business. Even those who had condemned crab-catching as a dirty sport bought them. They were delicious if you prepared them well. But these crabs that leaned uncertainly on the slope of the shore were different. They were very small and decorous, like cups and saucers which my mother bought and put away. You couldn't use them for drinking purposes. They were too delicate and decorous. These little crabs had that quality. Small, enchanting bits of furniture with which the shore was decorated. You wouldn't eat them although the meat might have been as delicious as that of the big village crabs, which were ugly and gross in their crawling movements.

Boy Blue didn't really want to eat one of these. He wanted to catch them as a kind of triumph. He could show what he had done after spending so many hours on the other side of the lighthouse. Catching things gave us little boys a great thrill. Sometimes we shot birds and carried them exposed in the palm of the hand. Everyone could see what we had done, meaning what he had achieved. It was like talking to the fisherman, or climbing a mountain which no one had hitherto dared ascend. The thrill of capturing something! It was wonderful! Boy Blue looked like a big crab crawling on all fours, and he made us laugh with the shift and shake of his slouching movements. The crabs dropped their eyes and remained still. It was always difficult to tell what a crab would do. Sometimes they would scamper wildly if you were a mile away, and at other times they would crouch and bundle themselves together the nearer you approached. They seemed to feel that they were unseen because their eyes were dropped level in the slot that contained them. Boy Blue lay flat on the sand with his hands stretched out full length. The crabs were trying to make a way in the sand. They had seen him but there was no great hurry in escaping. Perhaps the sand was their domain. They could appear and disappear at will while you waited and watched. His hands had them covered but there was no contact. The difficulties had only started. When you were catching a crab with bare hands you required great skill. You had to place

your thumb and index finger somewhere between the body
and the claws of the crab. That was very tricky, since the
crabs' claws were free like revolving chairs. They could spin,
it seemed, in all directions, and they raised and dropped
them to make any angle. Hundreds of boys were squeezed
time and again in their effort to trap the crabs barehanded. If
you missed the grip, or gripped a minute too soon the claws
had clinched you. And the claws cut like blades. You had to
know your job. You had to be a crab-catcher, as we would
say.

A master at the art, Boy Blue considered he was. He had
caught several in his time. The art had become a practised
routine. It was simply a matter of catching them. In this art
he carried the same assurance and command we had
noticed in the fisherman. He lay flat with his hands pressed
on the crabs' backs. He was trying to gather them up all
together. His thumb had found the accustomed spot
between the claw and the body of the crab. The crabs were
still but buckled tight, so it was difficult to strengthen the
grip. Sometimes they seemed to understand the game. They
remained still and stiffly buckled, and when you least
expected the claws flashed like edged weapons.

The waves came up and the sand slid back. It seemed they
would escape. If the waves came up again the sand would
be loosened and they could force a way easily into the sand.

Boy Blue had missed his grip. The wave came again and the sand sloped. Boy Blue slid back and the crabs were free from his grip. He propelled his feet in the sand in an attempt to heave himself forward. His weight pressed down. The wave receded and the sand shifted sharply. He came to a kneeling position and the sand slipped deeper. The crabs were safe. He threw his hand up and stood. The sand shifted under his feet and the waves hastening to the shore lashed him face downward. The salt stung his eyes and he groped to his feet. Another wave heaved and he tottered. The crabs! The crabs had disappeared. We could not understand what was happening. Boy Blue was laughing. It made us frighten the way he laughed. A wave wrenched him and now he was actually in the sea. We shivered, dumb. A wave pushed him up, and another completing the somersault plunged him down. He screamed and we screamed too. He was out of sight and we screamed with all the strength of our lungs. And the waves washed our screams up the shore. It was like a conspiracy of waves against the crab-catcher. We screamed and the fisherman came out from behind the lighthouse. We motioned to the spot where we had last seen Boy Blue. There was a faint scream in the air. We could not understand how it had happened. We could not follow the speed of the fisherman's movements. He had gathered up the net and tossed it in the sea over the area we had indicated. He hauled earnestly and the body of the net emerged with the strangest of all catches. Boy Blue was there. He was rolled up like a wet blanket. We were dumb with fright. He looked so impotent in the net. His eyes were bloodshot and his body heaved with a great flood of wind. He gasped and gasped, like a dog that had strained itself with too great speed in the chase. The fisherman hauled him up the beach and emptied the net as if it contained a useless dead thing. He looked at Boy Blue with a kind of disgust. Boy Blue was like a fly which had buzzed too long. You slapped it down and were sorry that you made such a mess of your hands. You might have left it. But you couldn't. It was unbearable. A necessary evil. Slapping it down. That's what it was. A necessary evil. The fisherman looked down at Boy Blue, unspeaking. There was no trace of what we would call bad temper. Just a kind of quiet disgust. Boy Blue sat silent, his teeth chattering and his whole body a shiver of flesh in the wind. We could not speak. We were afraid of the fisherman. The way he looked at us! He was like someone who had been sorry for what he did, and yet not sorry since he knew it had to be done. He looked so terribly repentant and at the same time there was an expression which we could not define. Under the marble eyes and the impenetrable stare there must have been something that cried out for life. He knew the catch was not a fish, but he hauled the net with the earnestness that could only have meant a desire beyond his control for the other's survival. Now he looked so terribly penitent. We were frightened.

"I should have let you drown," he snarled, and his voice held terror.

"Thank you, sir," Boy Blue said, catching his breath. It was the first time Boy Blue had spoken.

"By Christ, you should have drown," the fisherman snarled again.

"You mustn't say that," Boy Blue said. We were stunned by the impertinence of the words. But there couldn't have been impertinence. Boy Blue was shivering like a kitten that had had a bath.

"Why the heck shouldn't I have let you drown?" the fisherman shouted. It was the first thing he had said that made us think he was really human like us. The way he said it! He now looked angry.

"Tell me," he snapped. "Tell me to my face why I shouldn't have let you drown?"

"'Cause if I'd drown I wouldn't have been able to tell you thanks," Boy Blue said. He was serious and the fisherman walked back towards the lighthouse.

LOST IN THE CAVES

MARK TWAIN

Tom Sawyer and Becky Thatcher become separated from the picnic party in the caves, and find only Tom's enemy, the sinister Indian Joe.

NOW TO RETURN to Tom and Becky's share in the picnic. They tripped along the murky aisles with the rest of the company, visiting the familiar wonders of the cave – wonders dubbed with rather over-descriptive names, such as 'The Drawing room', 'The Cathedral', 'Aladdin's Palace', and so on. Presently the hide-and-seek frolicking began, and Tom and Becky engaged in it with zeal until the exertion began to grow a trifle wearisome; then they wandered down a sinuous avenue, holding their candles aloft and reading the tangled web-work of names, dates, post-office addresses, and mottoes with which the rocky walls had been frescoed (in candle smoke). Still drifting along and talking, they scarcely noticed that they were now in a part of the cave whose walls were not frescoed. They smoked their own names under an over-hanging shelf and moved on. Presently they came to a place where a little stream of water, trickling over a ledge and carrying a limestone sediment with it, had, in the slow-dragging ages, formed a laced and ruffled Niagara in gleaming and imperishable stone. Tom squeezed his small body behind it in order to illuminate it for Becky's gratification. He found that it curtained a sort of steep natural stair-way which was enclosed between narrow walls, and at once the ambition to be a discoverer seized him. Becky responded to his call, and they made a smoke mark for future guidance and started upon their quest. They wound this way and that, far down in to the secret depths of the cave, made another mark, and branched off in search of novelties to tell the upper world about.

In one place they found a spacious cavern, from whose ceiling depended a multitude of shining stalactites of the length and circumference of a man's leg; they walked all about it, wondering and admiring, and presently left it by one of the numerous passages that opened into it. This shortly brought them to a bewitching spring, whose basin was encrusted with a frostwork of glittering crystals; it was in the midst of a cavern whose walls were supported by many fantastic pillars which had been formed by the joining of great stalactites and stalagmites together, the result of the ceaseless water-drip of centuries. Under the roof vast knots of bats had packed themselves together, thousands in a bunch; the lights disturbed the creatures, and they came flocking down by hundreds, squeaking and darting furiously at the candles. Tom knew their ways and the danger of this sort of conduct. He seized Becky's hand and hurried her into the first corridor that offered; and none too soon, for a bat struck Becky's light out with its wing while she was passing out of the cavern. The bats chased the children a good distance; but the fugitives plunged into every new passage that offered, and at last got rid of the perilous things. Tom found a subterranean lake, shortly, which stretched its dim length away until its shape was lost in the shadows. He wanted to explore its borders, but concluded that it would be best to sit down and rest a while first. Now for the first time the deep stillness of the place laid a clammy hand upon the spirits of the children. Becky said:

"Why, I didn't notice, but it seems ever so long since I heard any of the others."

"Come to think, Becky, we are away down below them, and I don't know how far away north, or south, or east, or whichever it is. We couldn't hear them here."

Becky grew apprehensive.

"I wonder how long we've been down here, Tom. We better start back."

"Yes, I reckon we better. P'raps we better."

"Can you find the way, Tom? It's all a mixed-up crookedness to me."

"I reckon I could find it, but then the bats. If they put both our candles out it will be an awful fix. Let's try some other way, so as not to go through there."

"Well, but I hope we won't get lost. It would be so awful!" and the child shuddered at the thought of the dreadful possibilities.

They started through a corridor, and traversed it in silence a long way, glancing at each new opening, to see if there was anything familiar about the look of it; but they were all strange. Every time Tom made an examination, Becky would watch his face for an encouraging sign, and he would say cheerily:

"Oh, it's all right. This ain't the one, but we'll come to it right away!" But he felt less and less hopeful with each failure, and presently began to turn off into diverging avenues at sheer random, in the desperate hope of finding the one that was wanted. He still said it was "All right," but there was such a leaden dread at his heart, that the words had lost their ring, and sounded as if he had said, "All is lost!" Becky clung to his side in an anguish of fear, and tried hard to keep back the tears, but they would come. At last she said:

"Oh, Tom, never mind the bats; let's go back that way! We seem to get worse and worse off all the time."

Tom stopped.

"Listen!" said he.

Profound silence; silence so deep that even their breathings were conspicuous in the hush. Tom shouted. The call went echoing down the empty aisles, and died out in the distance in a faint sound that resembled a ripple of mocking laughter.

"Oh, don't do it again, Tom, it is too horrid," said Becky.

"It is horrid, but I better, Becky, they *might* hear us, you know," and he shouted again.

The 'might' was even a chillier horror than the ghostly laughter, it so confessed a perishing hope. The children stood still and listened; but there was no result. Tom turned upon the back tract at once, and hurried his steps. It was but a little while before a certain indecision in his manner revealed another fearful fact to Becky; he could not find his way back!

"Oh, Tom, you didn't make any marks!"

"Becky, I was such a fool! such a fool! I never thought we might want to come back! No, I can't find the way. It's all mixed up."

"Tom, Tom, we're lost! we're lost! We never, never can get out of this awful place! Oh, why did we ever leave the others?"

She sank to the ground, and burst into such a frenzy of crying that Tom was appalled with the idea that she might die, or lose her reason. He sat down by her and put his arms around her; she buried her face in his bosom, she clung to him, she poured out her terrors, her unavailing regrets, and the far echoes turned them all to jeering laughter. Tom begged her to pluck up hope again, and she said she could not. He fell to blaming and abusing himself for getting her into this miserable situation; this had a better effect. She said she would try to hope again, she would get up and follow wherever he might lead, if only he would not talk like that any more. For he was no more to blame than she, she said.

So they moved on again – aimlessly – simply at random – all they could do was to move, keep moving. For a little while hope made a show of reviving – not with any reason to back it, but only because it is its nature to revive when the spring has not been taken out of it by age and familiarity with failure.

By-and-by Tom took Becky's candle and blew it out. This

economy meant so much. Words were not needed. Becky understood, and her hope died again. She knew that Tom had a whole candle and three or four pieces in his pocket – yet he must economize.

By-and-by fatigue began to assert its claims; the children tried to pay no attention, for it was dreadful to think of sitting down when time was grown to be so precious; moving, in some direction, in any direction, was at least progress and might bear fruit; but to sit down was to invite death and shorten its pursuit.

At last Becky's frail limbs refused to carry her farther. She sat down. Tom rested with her, and they talked of home, and the friends there, and the comfortable beds, and above all, the light! Becky cried, and Tom tried to think of some way of comforting her, but all his encouragements were grown threadbare with use, and sounded like sarcasms. Fatigue bore so heavily upon Becky that she drowsed off to sleep. Tom was grateful. He sat looking into her drawn face and saw it grow smooth and natural under the influence of pleasant dreams; and by-and-by a smile dawned and rested there. The peaceful face reflected somewhat of peace and healing into his own spirit, and his thoughts wandered away to bygone times and dreamy memories. While he was deep in his musings, Becky woke up with a breezy little laugh: but it was stricken dead upon her lips, and a groan followed it.

"Oh, how *could* I sleep! I wish I never, never had waked! No, no, I don't, Tom! Don't look so! I won't say it again."

"I'm glad you slept, Becky; you'll feel rested, now, and we'll find the way out."

"We can try, Tom; but I've seen such a beautiful country in my dream. I reckon we are going there."

"Maybe not, maybe not. Cheer up, Becky, and let's go on trying."

They rose up and wandered along, hand in hand and hopeless. They tried to estimate how long they had been in the cave, but all they knew was that it seemed days and weeks, and yet it was plain that this could not be, for their candles were not gone yet.

A long time after this – they could not tell how long – Tom said they must go softly and listen for dripping water – they must find a spring. They found one presently, and Tom said it was time to rest again. Both were cruelly tired, yet Becky said she thought she could go a little farther. She was surprised to hear Tom dissent. She could not understand it. They sat down, and Tom fastened his candle to the wall in front of them with some clay. Thought was soon busy; nothing was said for some time. Then Becky broke the silence:

"Tom, I am so hungry!"

Tom took something out of his pocket.

"Do you remember this?" said he.

Becky almost smiled.

"It's our wedding-cake, Tom."

"Yes – I wish it was as big as a barrel, for it's all we've got."

"I saved it from the picnic for us to dream on, Tom, the way grown-up people do with wedding-cake – but it'll be our –"

She dropped the sentence where it was. Tom divided the cake, and Becky ate with good appetite, while Tom nibbled at his moiety. There was abundance of cold water to finish the feast with. By-and-by Becky suggested that they move on again. Tom was silent a moment. Then he said:

"Becky, can you bear it if I tell you something?"

Becky's face paled, but she said she thought she could.

"Well then, Becky, we must stay here, where there's water to drink. That little piece is our last candle!"

Becky gave loose to tears and wailings. Tom did what he could to comfort her, but with little effect. At length Becky said:

"Tom!"

"Well, Becky?"

"They'll miss us and hunt for us!"

"Yes, they will! Certainly they will!"

"Maybe they're hunting for us now, Tom?"

"Why, I reckon maybe they are! I hope they are."

"When would they miss us, Tom?"

"When they get back to the boat, I reckon."

"Tom, it might be dark, then – would they notice we hadn't come?"

"I don't know. But anyway, your mother would miss you as soon as they got home."

A frightened look in Becky's face brought Tom to his senses, and he saw that he had made a blunder. Becky was not to have gone home that night! The children became silent and thoughtful. In a moment a new burst of grief from Becky showed Tom that the thing in his mind had struck hers also – that the Sabbath morning might be half spent before Mrs Thatcher discovered that Becky was not at Mrs Harper's. The children fastened their eyes upon their bit of candle and watched it melt slowly and pitilessly away; saw the half-inch of wick stand alone at last: saw the feeble flame rise and fall, rise and fall, climb the thin column of smoke, linger at its top a moment, and then – the horror of utter darkness reigned.

How long afterwards it was that Becky came to a slow consciousness that she was crying in Tom's arms, neither could tell. All that they knew was that after what seemed a mighty stretch of time, both awoke out of a dead stupor of sleep, and resumed their miseries once more. Tom said it might be Sunday now – maybe Monday. He tried to get Becky to talk, but her sorrows were too oppressive, all her hopes were gone. Tom said that they must have been missed long ago, and no doubt the search was going on. He would shout, and maybe someone would come. He tried it; but in the darkness the distant echoes sounded so hideously that he tried it no more.

The hours wasted away, and hunger came to torment the captives again. A portion of Tom's half of the cake was left; they divided and ate it. But they seemed hungrier than before. The poor morsel of food only whetted desire.

By-and-by Tom said:

"*Sh!* Did you hear that?"

Both held their breath and listened. There was a sound like the faintest far-off shout. Instantly Tom answered it, and leading Becky by the hand, started groping down the corridor in its direction. Presently he listened again; again the sound was heard, and apparently a little nearer.

"It's them!" said Tom; "they're coming! Come along, Becky – we're all right now!"

The joy of the prisoners was almost overwhelming. Their speed was slow, however, because pitfalls were somewhat common, and had to be guarded against. They shortly came to one, and had to stop. It might be three feet deep, it might be a hundred – there was no passing it, at any rate. Tom got down on his breast, and reached as far down as he could. No bottom. They must stay there and wait until the searchers came. They listened; evidently the distant shoutings were growing more distant! A moment or two more, and they had gone altogether. The heart-sinking misery of it! Tom whooped until he was hoarse, but it was of no use. He talked hopefully to

Becky; but an age of anxious waiting passed and no sound came again.

The children groped their way back to the spring. The weary time dragged on; they slept again, and awoke famished and woe-stricken. Tom believed it must be Tuesday by this time.

Now an idea struck him. There were some side-passages near at hand. It would be better to explore some of these than bear the weight of the heavy time in idleness. He took a kite-line from his pocket, tied it to a projection, and he and Becky started, Tom in the lead, unwinding the line as he groped along. At the end of twenty steps the corridor ended in a 'jumping-off place'. Tom got down on his knees and felt below, and then as far around the corner as he could reach with his hands conveniently; he made an effort to stretch yet a little further to the right, and at that moment, not twenty yards away, a human hand, holding a candle, appeared from behind a rock! Tom lifted up a glorious shout, and instantly that hand was followed by the body it belonged to – Injun Joe's! Tom was paralysed; he could not move. He was vastly gratified the next moment to see the 'Spaniard' take to his heels and get himself out of sight. Tom wondered that Joe had not recognized his voice and come over and killed him for testifying in court. But the echoes must have disguised the voice. Without doubt that was it, he reasoned. Tom's fright weakened every muscle in his body. He said to himself that if he had strength enough to get back to the spring he would stay there, and nothing should tempt him to run the risk of meeting Injun Joe again. He was careful to keep from Becky what it was he had seen. He told her he had only shouted "for luck".

But hunger and wretchedness rise superior to fears in the long run. Another tedious wait at the spring, and another long sleep brought changes. The children awoke, tortured with a raging hunger. Tom believed it must be Wednesday or Thursday, or even Friday or Saturday, now, and that the search had been given over. He proposed to explore another passage. He felt willing to risk Injun Joe and all other terrors. But Becky was very weak. She had sunk into a dreary apathy, and would not be roused. She said she would wait, now, where she was, and die – it would not be long. She told Tom to go with the kite-line and explore if he chose; but she implored him to come back every little while and speak to her; and she made him promise that when the awful time came, he would stay by her and hold her hand until all was over. Tom kissed her, with a choking sensation in his throat, and made a show of being confident of finding the searchers or an escape from the cave; then he took the kite-line in his hand and went groping down one of the passages on his hands and knees, distressed with hunger and sick with bodings of coming doom.

Tuesday afternoon came, and waned to the twilight. The village of St Petersburg still mourned. The lost children had not been found. Public prayers had been offered up for them, and many and many a private prayer that had the petitioner's whole heart in it; but still no good news came from the cave. The majority of the searchers had given up the quest and gone back to their daily avocations, saying that it was plain the children could never be found. Mrs Thatcher was very ill, and a great part of the time delirious. People said it was heart-breaking to hear her call her child, and raise her head and listen a whole minute at a time, then lay it wearily down again with a moan. Aunt Polly had drooped into a settled melancholy, and her grey hair had grown almost white. The village went to its rest on Tuesday night, sad and forlorn.

Away in the middle of the night a wild peal burst from the village bells, and in a moment the streets were swarming with frantic, half-clad people, who shouted, "Turn out! turn out! they're found! they're found!" Tin pans and horns were added to the din, the population massed itself and moved towards the river, met the children coming in an open carriage drawn by shouting citizens, thronged around it, joined its homeward march, and swept magnificently up the main street roaring huzza after huzza!

The village was illuminated; nobody went to bed again; it was the greatest night the little town had ever seen. During the first half-hour a procession of villagers filed through Judge Thatcher's house, seized the saved ones and kissed them, squeezed Mrs Thatcher's hand, tried to speak but couldn't, and drifted out raining tears all over the place.

Aunt Polly's happiness was complete, and Mrs Thatcher's nearly so. It would be complete, however, as soon as the

messenger despatched with the great news to the cave should get the word to her husband.

Tom lay upon a sofa with an eager auditory about him, and told the history of the wonderful adventure, putting in many striking additions to adorn it withal; and closed with a description of how he left Becky and went on an exploring expedition; how he followed two avenues as far as his kite-line would reach; how he followed a third to the fullest stretch of the kite-line, and was about to turn back when he glimpsed a far-off speck that looked like daylight; dropped the line and groped towards it, pushed his head and shoulders through a small hole and saw the broad Mississippi rolling by! And if it had only happened to be night he would not have seen that speck of daylight, and would not have explored that passage any more! He told how he went back for Becky and broke the good news, and she told him not to fret her with such stuff, for she was tired, and knew she was going to die, and wanted to. He described how he laboured with her and convinced her, and how she almost died for joy when she had groped to where she actually saw the blue speck of daylight; how he pushed his way out of the hole and then helped her out; how they sat there and cried for gladness; how some men came along in a skiff, and Tom hailed them and told them their situation and their famished condition; how the men didn't believe the wild tale at first, "because," said they, "you are five miles down the river below the valley the cave is in;" then took them aboard, rowed to a house, gave them supper, made them rest till two or three hours after dark, and then brought them home.

A HUNDRED MILLION FRANCS

PAUL BERNA

A gang of young French children defend a factory that makes party novelties against an adult gang who have stolen their 'horse' – a soap-box on wheels. The youngsters thought it was only play-money that they had found in the joke-factory, but . . .

THE GRILL THAT separated the stock-room from the rest of the building was made of solid slats of wood that ran from floor to ceiling. The double door, strengthened with wooden cross-beams, was fastened top and bottom by two thick bolts which could not be reached from outside. But it still wasn't enough to stop the intruders.

Without wasting a second they all fell to work, piling boxes of carnival novelties up against the partition, the heaviest at the bottom as a firm foundation for the barricade and the lighter ones tossed in showers on the top. As they fell some of them broke open and the place was soon festooned with a tangle of paper chains of all colours, plumes of horse-hair, chinese umbrellas, cardboard crowns, jacks-in-the-box, streamers of artificial flowers, a snow of spangles, armfuls of gazookas and rattles, castanets, false beards, false noses, false teeth, and all the thousand and one treasures of this Ali Baba's cave of a store-room.

An appalling crash and the tinkle of broken glass came from the neighbouring room. A flash-light beam played furtively upon the bluish glass of the roof; heavy boots clumped across the concrete floor, and slowly drew near the store-room.

"One more door," said Fernand, "and then we'll see what these toy thieves really look like."

"Out with the candles," hissed Gaby, trembling with excitement. "Get back to the far end of the store, behind the last pile of boxes. If anyone laughs I'll do them."

Bottling their laughter the children tiptoed off, tripping over the oddments that littered the passage down the middle. From one end of the room to the other the cases of goods were carefully stacked head high, leaving a gap about a yard wide between each pile. These cardboard fortifications not only gave an illusion of safety, but as Gaby said, could easily be pushed over if it came to a tussle, and so create the most glorious chaos.

The last door made the toughs sweat a bit. It was metal-sheathed and Gaby had securely double-locked it. They had to join forces to smash it in. They used a work-bench which they swung like a battering-ram, backwards and forwards, their curses setting the rhythm. All at once one of the panels gave way completely and most of the door-frame with it. The crash stifled the giggles of Berthe and Mélie, set off by the cascade of paper streamers that had fallen out of the half-open cupboard and buried them up to their necks.

Gaby and Fernand were side by side, entrenched behind the first wall of boxes. By pushing two of them out of the pile they had made themselves a peep-hole. On the other side of the slatted partition they saw the toughs come into the room, one behind the other. The dancing light of a torch flashed on the burly forms and now caught one scowling face and now another. The one in the lead put his foot in the pig's-head mask, which happened to be lying in his path. He tripped and measured his length on the floor, bringing down with him a pile of paint-cans in a glorious clatter. He spat and swore, and, cursing his comrades and puffing and blowing, he heaved himself to his feet. Quite by accident he got a long black beard stuck to the end of his nose. This mishap cheered Gaby's gang; the tension had been growing unbearable.

"You won't get anywhere until you get some decent light," came a deep voice in the background. "The fuse-box is out here in the entrance hall. Knock the front off and put in some fresh wires. No one will see us. The nearest house is a good half-mile away."

Two minutes later a harsh light was playing from the bulbs that ran the length of the roof upon the grand chaos the children's visits had made, and on the fading treasures of the factory. Satisfied, the crooks dashed forward to the partition. There were five of them. Fernand and Gaby had no difficulty in picking out Pepé and Ugly in their leather jackets, and a little behind them, as though rather unsure of himself, the tall shape of Roublot. The other two wore heavy overcoats, the collars turned up so that their faces could not be seen properly.

Roughly, Ugly rattled the slats, muttering under his breath.

"Those little blighters have locked themselves in behind there. Well, we'll soon shift 'em!"

He went for the door with a crow-bar. But the cross-beams were thick and the bolts were solid steel, and the door held firm. Red with anger, Ugly hurled his tool away, and poking his face through the slats he yelled: "You in there! Get this door open, and make it snappy, or I'll wring your blasted necks!"

"Open up, you little ruffians!" added Pepé.

Nothing stirred in the store-room.

"That's not the way to talk to children," said one of the men in overcoats, quietly. (He seemed to be the leader.) "Here, let me."

Then, pushing the two others aside, he looked inquisitively between the slats. A solitary bulb hung over the door and dimly lit the long store-room with its grey steel cupboards and regular walls of boxes across the room.

"Come, come, come, come, come!" he sang out, as though calling in the hens for feeding. "Don't be naughty. Open the door like good children and no one will be cross. Here's a hundred francs for the first one to come out."

There was not a sound from the store. No one wanted the hundred francs, and Tatave for one would have willingly given a hundred thousand to be somewhere else. Zidore and Juan had just found a box of bangers in their 'wall'. These bangers were little round paper balls filled with sand and holding a detonator cap. A hard throw would send them off with a fine explosion. Taking a handful each, they jumped up and threw them over the top of the boxes. They made a terrific bang-bang as they went off against the partition. It was like a burst of tommy-gun fire. Taken by surprise, the men instinctively drew back, shielding their heads with their arms. At the

same time Gaby and Fernand leapt back to rejoin their friends.

"Help yourselves!" Zidore whispered. "But let's shift a bit, or they'll spot us!"

The five crooks, boiling with rage, once more returned to the partition, this time with pistols drawn.

"Well, if you like that sort of game," the leader shouted at the children, "we'll join in too!"

. And sliding his hand between the slats, he blindly let loose a volley of shots. The force of the bullets hitting and rebounding off the cupboards opened their doors and poured their contents on to the children crouching below. The crash of the explosions only roused the children still more, and Berthe and Mélie grabbed their share of bangers. One after the other the two girls, Fernand and Gaby, Zidore and Juan, hurled their grenades against the partition. One moment they were on their feet and the next they were full length in the heaps of crêpe-paper that carpeted the floor.

Roublot and Ugly slipped out into the next-door workshop. They came back dragging the bench which they had used before as a battering-ram. All together the five of them picked up the heavy table and brought it crashing against the door. The panels cracked and part of the barricade the children had made collapsed under the shock.

A real storm of bangers burst with a blinding flash against the partition. The second blow from the battering-ram tore the bolt out of the bottom of the door, smashed in the lower panel, and brought down a whole mound of boxes. All the children were now on their feet and, throwing caution to the winds, they hurled their bombs by the handful, harassing the five men as they drew back for their last assault.

"What can Marion be doing?" muttered Fernand as he scraped the last handful of bangers from the bottom of the box.

Marion jumped over the low wall at the end of the yard and landed as lightly as a cat on the other side. It was very dark by now, but a fresh fall of snow covered the ground and by its pale glitter you could make out the mounds and hollows in the ground, above all the dangerous bomb-craters that riddled the bottom of the field beside the railway tracks. Marion took to her heels and dashed into the darkness, heading for the ghostly mass of the rusty old Black Cow faintly outlined by the lights of the town behind it.

The snow went on falling gently, but the wind had fallen away. The noise of the traffic died down towards Triage and gradually this little corner of the suburbs became as quiet as the country.

When she reached the old engine, Marion stopped to rest for a second. Then she put two fingers between her teeth, took a deep breath, and began to whistle. Her shrill, wavering call travelled across the Clos Pecqueux, making itself heard above the roar of the traffic on the main roads and penetrated the streets, the alleys, the back-yards, the gardens, the sheds, and the barns.

Turning towards the lights of Louvigny that shone in her face, Marion whistled with all her might, not weakening but rather gaining power from the echo from the embankment, which prolonged the sinister note. Through the bitter night, she whistled up help for the children from the rue des Petits-Pauvres.

Butor and Fanfan, Marion's two farm dogs, were the first to hear her urgent summons. They were hunting a cat at the head of the rue de la Vache Noire. The hair on their necks rose and, leaving the big tom, they cleared the barbed wire at one bound and hurled themselves into the darkness of the Clos Pecqueux. At the foot of the rue des Petits-Pauvres, Marion's twelve patients snored on, and the alert Fifi was the only one to jump the fence and run like a hare towards the Black Cow.

Close on her heels came the three aristocrats of the rue Cécile – Hugo, Fritz and César. Shoulder to shoulder they took the corner of the cross-roads and vanished as fast as they had come. Dingo, Cobbler Gally's old spaniel, got under way more slowly, crossed the road behind them, and slipped under the barbed wire with an angry growl. One after the other, Pipotte, old Monsieur Gédéon's bitch, and Moko, the fox-terrier belonging to the Babin family, came down the rue des Petits-Pauvres, and after them five ugly mongrels from Cité Ferrand: Mataf, Doré, Jeremie, Ursule, and Drinette. The whole mob of them turned the corner at full speed, heads down, never a bark, and nearly knocked down the solitary pedestrian who was coming up the Ponceau road. Mustafa, the one-eyed Alsatian from the Bar de l'Auvergnat, and Zanzi, Madame Louvrier's poodle, came galloping along with Émile and Fido, the two retrievers owned by Monsieur Manteau, the Mayor of Louvigny. And those four nobly swelled the muster.

All the while Marion whistled.

Gamin, Monsieur Joye's black-and-white terrier, soon turned the corner of the rue Aubertin and raced up the rue de la Vache Noire slightly ahead of the reinforcements from Louvigny-Cambrouse. The latter came helter-skelter across the main road, not bothering about the glaring headlights or the screeching brakes.

Mignon, the bulldog belonging to Maubert the small-holder, brought with him the rough-and-tough mongrels from the neighbourhood of les Maches: Filon, Canard, Betasse, Flip, and Briquet. And behind them came the farm dogs from the Bas-Louvigny, dark, shaggy, snarling, snapping brutes: Raleur, and Nougat, limping Croquant (though he didn't limp now) and yellow-eyed Charlot – scarred, and with most of his ears chewed off – Taquin, a mangy beast, and Canon the chicken-thief. This robber band came pattering along the tarmac of the main road. It was a wonderful sight to see the entire dog population of Louvigny in migration from one side of the town to the other.

And it was even better to see the toffs of the Quartier-Neuf joining in the game and sending such clipped and

combed champions as Otto de la Ville-Neuberg du Pacq des Primevères, the boxer whose pedigree covered four whole pages, and whose daily dish was a pound of best-quality minced beef; Bébé, the black Schnauzer with eyes like a goat; Hubert, the boar-hound, four times a medal winner, who could jump any wall; Popoff, the greyhound, once famous in the stadium; Zoum, the griffon, with an insatiable appetite for slippers and soft furnishings; and then five little dogs of all shapes and sizes, all a little over-plump, and all highly scented. Every one of them had passed through Marion's hands for some cure or other. Yes, the toffs of the Quartier-Neuf were hastening eagerly to the rallying place.

And still Marion went on whistling in the darkness of the Clos Pecqueux. A faint echo even reached the little houses of Petit-Louvigny and the Faubourg-Bacchus, and all at once every dog in the place seemed to go mad: rag-pickers' mongrels for the most part, good for nothing and living like outlaws on the fringes of the shopping streets. Leaving whatever they were doing, the rag-tag and bob-tail came out of the wooden huts and the waste land, entered the town-centre, crossed the Grand Rue and the rue Piot, turned up the rue des Alliés, and dashed full-cry down the rue des Petits-Pauvres, quite blocking the pavement. Pipi, Juan's lemon-and-white fox-terrier, was leading the pack with old Chable's dog, Arthur, a short-legged mongrel with a jackal's

127

head, a coat as rough as a bass-broom, and one eye black and one eye blue. Then came Caillette, Frisé, Loupiotte l'Apache, Chopine, old Zigon's bitch, Golo, the Lariqués' lurcher, the old pug Adolf, Polyte, Bidasse, Gros-Père, and a dozen other flea-ridden curs, who changed name and home regularly once a week.

Planted beneath the threatening bulk of the Black Cow, Marion was still whistling as hard as she could when the first dogs reached her. She had half seen them in the darkness of Clos Pecqueux, wave upon wave of them, racing silently towards her. Not one of them gave tongue – Marion didn't allow that – and their feet pattered on the ground like a rain-storm. In a few seconds she found herself hemmed in by a growling mass that eagerly twisted and turned to touch her friendly hand or sniff her coat. The more dogs there were about her, the gentler and more caressing her whistle grew. Louvigny-Cambrouse and the Quartier-Neuf arrived almost together, and then came the flea-ridden rabble from the Faubourg-Bacchus.

Every so often the beam of a distant headlight caught the group, and hundreds of eyes gleamed red and green around her, like so many fire-flies. The dogs whimpered with delight, and occasionally one or the other of them would give a plaintive little whine.

"Whisht!" said Marion, throwing wide her arms, "here, here!"

The dogs closed round her, leaping, gazing adoringly up at her. Marion held out her arms, recognizing them by touch, stroking noses, patting backs, and calling them by name as she did so.

Then with a sharp call of "Come!" she broke through them and set off running towards the bottom of the Clos Pecqueux. Obediently the dogs panted after her. The whole pack threaded their way through the narrow lane that led into the Ponceau road. As the dogs eagerly crowded after Marion, an express thundered along the embankment in a shimmer of golden lights.

Her pace slackened when she approached the factory. The splintered gates yawned black, but there was a glow of light above the workshop roof. From the depths of the building came a series of muffled thuds. She went in – or rather, she was pushed in by the wild rush of the dogs, who hurled themselves panting from room to room.

A cloud of acrid smoke hung above the end workshop. The partition was still holding – but only just. The five crooks were swinging their battering-ram for the final blow. With a crash, one half of the door fell in and brought down with it the barricade of boxes.

"Hey!" called Marion.

The astonished men turned, and their hands hung useless and their jaws dropped to see the girl and her sixty silent, straining hounds standing behind them. The dogs were waiting as though they were held back only by some invisible leash.

"Go on!" cried Marion in a shrill voice. "Catch 'em! Pull 'em down! Rotten swine who pinch kids' toys in the rue des Petits-Pauvres!"

With a joyful bound the dogs fell to work.

THE SOUND OF PROPELLERS

CLIVE KING

*Murugan, brought from India to be educated in England, desperately
needs to get home to save his brother from serious trouble. He happens
to unmask a spy, but the gratitude of the authorities doesn't extend to
flying him home. Was it the mysterious spy who left the door open when
he tries to stow away on the fantastic pickaback aircraft?*

> *Red sails in the sunset,*
> *Far over the sea,*
> *Oh, carry my loved one*
> *Home safely to me!*

THE MUSIC TAILED off in a mournful moan.

Barbara said, "For goodness' sake wind it up,
Mouse!"

William furiously wound the handle of the little square
clockwork gramophone. The singer perked up, but sounded
a bit husky.

"It needs a new gramophone needle," said Barbara.

"You need a new record," William said.

"I like that record," Barbara said. So did I. I liked sitting in
the cosy room in the Woods' house, which they still called
the nursery. I liked being asked home by the Woods family. I
liked William. I liked Barbara, especially.

She was looking at that newspaper.

"Do you really want to fly to India?" she asked me.

"Yes," I said. "They asked me what I wanted as a reward and I said I wanted to fly to India. I – I want to see my family. But it was very kind of them to let me have that short trip."

"They asked you what you wanted and then they didn't give it to you?" she demanded.

"Yes, I asked too much."

Barbara threw down the paper angrily.

"I think it's a *swizz*! I think they're being *mean*!"

"Perhaps it is not possible, what I asked."

"But Mercury is going to fly to India," she said.

William asked her scornfully, "Who told you that one, Bats?"

"Oh, I get to hear things, at home," she tossed her head. "I'm pretty sure of this one."

We sat and listened to that record again from the beginning. Or, rather, I didn't listen. My mind was churning. Mercury was flying all the way to India. Madras in a couple of days, Mr Woods had said. So did all my calculations – but no, it was no use my thinking about it. I'd had my reward.

Barbara lifted the arm off the gramophone.

"You'll have to be a stowaway," she said.

"What is stow-a-way?" I could hardly even say the word. I was still having trouble with my English W's, and this word had two in it.

"Oh, he doesn't even know the *word*! Sometimes I think you're useless, Mugwumps!"

I turned away from her, pretending to feel very hurt. But I wasn't. She was talking to me as she talked to her own brother. That made us equals.

"Sorry!" she said, and she gave my knee a quick pat. "Look. There's Mercury down on the river. It'll fly to India *tomorrow*! All you've got to do is get on board and stay there. I bet *I* could!"

It seemed simple. Too simple?

"What do you think Mouse?" she turned to her brother.

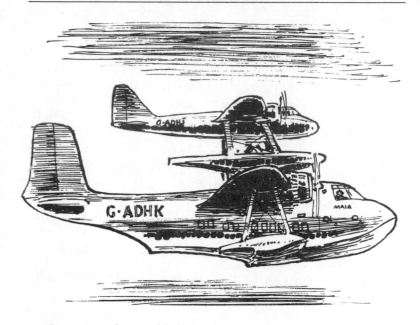

"I suppose he could. But it's term-time."

"Oh, *bloody term-time!*" she swore. I didn't like her using such words.

"It's running away from school," said Mouse. "They can expel you for that."

"People who run away don't want to stay, do they? All we've got to do is get up early. We can pack you some pie or something from the larder. You won't need a lot of food for less than two days. Then we can take the dinghy out and pretend we're going for an early morning row. We'll get you on board somehow." She was speaking quietly now, hatching her plot.

"Suppose it doesn't work?" Mouse said.

"If it doesn't work, it doesn't work. But it'll work if we don't funk it."

I had the feeling that things were out of my hands, with this forceful girl in charge. I couldn't believe it would happen, even though I wanted it to. I just went along with

Barbara's detailed plans. She would borrow Cook's alarm clock while she wasn't looking – though I was sure I wouldn't be able to sleep a wink myself. I would have to put on all the warm clothes I'd got, because they thought the baggage-hold would get very cold. The family had a little boat down by the river, and they would row me out to Mercury-Maia, moored in the stream. And that was it.

I felt I ought to go round saying good-bye to everybody, as I'd done when I left India, but of course I couldn't. We had to pretend to Mr and Mrs Woods that nothing was happening. It was difficult to keep talking about other things. When Barbara and William asked to go to bed early, Mrs Woods looked quite worried.

"You're not sickening for something, are you?" she demanded.

Mouse and I were to sleep in the same bedroom. Or, rather, we agreed we would rest in our beds and keep awake until it was time to go. I looked in my little suitcase to see what warm clothes I'd brought. If I'd known I was packing for such an adventure I could have brought sports sweaters and things. But I'd have to make do with a spare woolly vest and two pairs of socks.

"You could wear your pajama underneath your suit," Mouse suggested.

"My pyjamas," I corrected him. We both giggled, remembering my first night at school. We got into our beds and Mouse turned off the light.

"We can't leave the light on all night," he said. "Mum and Dad might suspect something."

We settled down in the dark to our murmured conversation.

"Even if it does work, won't you get into trouble, you and Barbara?" I asked.

"I dare say. But they can't eat us."

"Won't they search for me, as soon as they notice I'm missing?"

"Mmm. We'll think of some story. I'll say you went back to school for something – for your cough medicine."

133

"Say good-bye to Stodge for me, when I'm gone," I asked him. "Tell him I'll bring him back some burphy."

"What's burphy?" I heard him giggle in the dark.

"A kind of sweet. It will make him even fatter."

"So you *are* coming back, then?"

"How can I tell? I may not get another free trip."

"I suppose you may not want to, once you're in India. Do you have to go to school there?"

"You are lucky if your parents can send you to school."

"I don't think it's lucky. Anyway, hasn't your father got enough money?"

It was strange – we knew each other quite well now, but we hardly ever talked about these things.

"My father is dead," I told him. He was silent for a bit.

"Sorry. Was he a rich man?"

"He had a catamaran."

"What's that?"

"A kind of boat."

"So he was a shipowner?"

"Not exactly. A catamaran is five logs tied together, and a sail. My father went fishing in the monsoon, and never came back. That's why my mother became a Christian."

"Sorry – I don't understand."

"My father believed in the Indian gods – Vishnu, and Krishna, and Ganesha the elephant god, and Murugan after whom I am named. But they did not look after him well, did they? Someone told my mother that Jesus would look after her and her sons better. And it is true, isn't it? Look, I am having this excellent education in Rochester! But my brother needs my help and I must go to him."

How much should I tell him about my brother? Would he understand? But something about William's steady breathing told me that he was already asleep. And with nobody to keep me awake, I went off to sleep myself.

Deep, deep sleep. Some confused dreams, about a flying-boat made of logs tied together with rope. A man like a black bat in a wading-suit was untying the ropes . . .

Someone was shaking my arm as I tried to snuggle down into my supersoft warm bed. Was I late for school breakfast, for shoe-polishing, for a day of lessons? I opened my eyes to darkness, except for the wavering beam of a little electric torch. A figure was bending over me, and the light fell on a pair of riding jodhpurs and thick socks.

"Wake up! Wake *up*!" came Barbara's sharp whisper. "It's twenty to five."

The air in the bedroom was cold. Oh, no! It all came back to me, yesterday's silly plot about flying to India. But it was one thing to hatch a plot in a cosy nursery. Did they really think I was going to get up in the freezing dark and *do* it? That was something quite different. I groaned and wriggled back under the blankets.

But Barbara was over by William's bed now, giving him a shake.

"Come *on*, William! Get yourself dressed and see that Murugan does too. I'll be down in the kitchen."

At school William was always one of the slowest in the morning. But at his sister's bidding he had switched on his torch and rolled out of bed. Now he was over by mine, pulling all the bedclothes off.

"But I'm not going!" I protested.

"Rot!" he said. "Get dressed!"

It was no use arguing with these two. They were determined to start their adventure, whatever I felt about it. I got up and put on as many clothes as I could find.

By the light of his torch William and I crept very quietly downstairs past his parents' bedroom, and down to the kitchen. There was a smell of cold grease, and Barbara's torchlight flickering about as she put things into a brown paper bag on the scrubbed kitchen table. William's torch shone on the dog, looking up and wagging his tail hopefully.

"Cold cooked sausages, chocolate biscuits, and an orange," Barbara whispered. "I'm afraid it's all I can find. Hadn't you better have something to eat before you go?"

Impossible! My mouth was as dry as if I was dying of

135

thirst, and my stomach was churning. I drank two glasses of water at the kitchen tap, and stuffed the paper bag into my overcoat pocket. William handed me another little bag.

"What's that?" Barbara asked.

"Survival kit," William whispered. "Pencil and paper, a pen knife, a torch, a piece of string and some money. It's a lucky rupee Dad gave me – that's Indian, isn't it?"

I thanked him and put the bag into my other pocket. My baggage for a six-thousand-mile journey! I still couldn't believe it was happening.

Barbara had an iron key in her hand. She moved towards the back door. "Let's go, then," she said quietly. "Come on, Wat, boy!"

"He's not taking the dog to India!" William protested.

"Idiot!" Barbara hissed. "If we leave Wat behind he'll bark to come with us and wake up the whole house. We've got to take him."

She unlocked and opened the back door, and the east wind hit us. I wrapped my school scarf round my head and face. As we stole across the back lawn the stars were twinkling overhead. There was a glare in the city sky from the all-night street-lighting, but no sign of dawn. My heart began to pump with excitement. After all, this *was* an adventure.

"Oars!" William suddenly hissed in the silence.

"Eh?" Barbara queried.

"In the summer house," William whispered. "We'll need oars, for the dinghy." He went off to the other side of the lawn and came back after a time with a bundle of long things in his arms. He gave me two oars to carry. Barbara shone a light on the other things.

"We don't need *fishing rods*, stupid!" she hissed.

"I thought we'd better take them."

"Oh, all *right*, then, take them."

From the way they were snapping at each other I could see they were as nervous as I was.

We went out through the garden gate and took the

footpath down to the river. There were street-lights near the factory, and beyond them the river was vast and dark.

"There she is," William hissed, pointing with his fishing rods towards the water. We stopped on the slope. I could just make out the crazy Meccano structure of Mercury-Maia, moored in the stream. How could that thing fly me to India? I must be dreaming, and I would soon wake up.

On the riverside road to the factory our footsteps echoed back to us from brick walls. William flapped his hand to us, signalling us to stop. We halted and listened. Footsteps, heavy and slow, continued to sound. They weren't ours. Round a corner came a tall dark figure in a cape. A policeman.

Oh, well, that was that. What were you supposed to say? *It's a fair cop?* We'd all get sent straight to Borstal – though perhaps not Barbara.

The policeman paced steadily towards us and shone an electric lantern on our faces. Barbara's bright voice rang out.

"Hello, it's Constable Heaver! Keeping a good watch on the factory, Constable Heaver!"

"Well I never! It's Miss Woods, isn't it?" said the policeman. "And young master William." He stared suspiciously at my face, all wrapped up, but I decided not to unwrap it. "What may you be doing, out so early?"

"Daddy always likes an early start for a fishing trip," Barbara chirped. "If you see him with a bucket of maggots, tell him we've gone on to the boat, will you, please?"

The constable looked at William. "Got the rest of your gear, I see. All right, Miss Barbara, I'll keep a look out for your Dad." He stooped stiffly to pat the dog. "Don't get up to mischief before he comes, will you?" And with a last suspicious glance at me he went on his way.

When we'd got far enough in the

other direction Bats and Mouse exploded into relieved giggles.

"Bucket of maggots!" William spluttered. "The lies you tell, Bats!"

"I didn't tell any lies," Barbara insisted. "I said *if* he met Daddy with a bucket of maggots – well, he'd know what to say."

What a family! They had no respect for anybody, not even policemen.

"It was my fishing rods that made him believe you, though," William said.

"I suppose it *was* a good idea to bring them," his sister gave way.

Away from the factory there was a little jetty where shadowy dinghies were tied up. In midstream the dancing water reflected starlight and the street-lamps of Strood. But at this end of the jetty – the two torches shone down on boats stuck in black mud.

"Oh, *no!*" The laughter died out of Barbara's voice. "You didn't think of the tide, did you, William?"

"Nor did you!" William snapped back. "It's right out. What do we do now? Wait for it to come in?"

I looked down at the slimy, smelly mud, sorry for my friends and their plans that had gone wrong. Perhaps *I* should have thought of the tide. It's easy enough to calculate high water if you know when the moon rises . . . But perhaps we could go back to bed now.

William had wandered on to the end of the jetty. Now he was calling back to us.

"Come on! There's water at this end. And someone's boat."

Barbara and the dog ran to the end of the jetty. I followed. They were shining their torches down on to a heavy, clumsy-looking dinghy tied up to the bottom of an iron ladder. It was floating in a little muddy channel.

"Are you going to steal a boat?" I protested.

"People do borrow boats," Mouse said. "We'll get it back, I suppose."

"It'll do," Barbara said, and began to climb down the

ladder. She pulled the boat towards her by the rope, and got in.

"Pass down the oars and things," she ordered. We did that easily enough.

"What about the dog?" William asked from the jetty.

"Oh, why did we have to bring him?" Barbara groaned.

"It wasn't my idea," her brother snapped.

"Get half-way down the ladder, Mouse," Barbara ordered. "Murugan can pass him down to you and you can pass him to me."

That was easier said than done. I don't think the dog liked the idea of water at all. He wriggled and whined and I didn't know what to hold on by. William nearly dropped him, and he yelped as Barbara dumped him in the boat.

"*Shut up, Wat!*" said Barbara between clenched teeth. "Next time we'll leave you *behind!*"

Next time? I wondered how often they thought they'd do this sort of thing.

It was my turn to go down that ladder. As I got to the bottom Barbara called out another order.

"Let go the painter!"

"I beg your pardon?" I had to say.

I was hanging on to the slimy iron ladder, and it was freezing my fingers.

"The *rope*, Mugwumps," William said. "Undo it!"

My fingers struggled with the soggy rope in the cold iron ring. At last it came undone and flopped into the water. William hung on to the ladder as I got into the boat. My foot went into an inch or two of icy water sloshing around in the bottom.

"Can you row, Murugan?" Barbara asked me.

Well, yes, I wasn't a fisherman's son for nothing. I had helped to man the big rowing-sweeps on the river boats at home. You stood up facing forwards and pushed on the handle of the long oar. So I took an oar and, standing in the dinghy, looked for somewhere to lodge it. The little boat rocked.

"For goodness' sake sit *down*!" Barbara hissed. "If you don't know anything about rowing, say so!"

I wasn't even sure I liked this girl any more.

She snatched the oar from me and sat down facing the back of the boat. William took the other oar and did the same on the other side. It seemed a funny way to move a boat – they couldn't even see where they were going. Did *they* know what they were doing?

But it seemed to work. There was just enough water in that narrow channel to float the boat out towards the main stream. Then we were out on the choppy water, and brother and sister had to work hard together to keep the boat moving against wind and tide. All I could do was keep my eyes on the shadowy outline of Mercury-Maia, and tell them "This way a bit!" or "That way a bit!" to keep them on course.

"Are you sure you can see it?" Barbara panted, between strokes.

"Yes, it's got a light on," I told her. "Do you think that means there's someone there?"

"Don't think so," she puffed. "They've got to have a light – to stop boats bumping into it."

But after a while the light went out. Somebody must have switched it off. So there must be somebody there. I told Barbara.

"What do we do if there *is* someone there?" I asked Barbara.

"Carry on fishing," she said, saving her breath.

We were getting nearer. The black shape of Mercury-Maia merged with the mass of Rochester Bridge behind it. I couldn't be sure which I was looking at. Was that a dark figure walking along Maia's wing? Or was it somebody on the bridge?

The darkness and the reflections of the lamps on the bridge kept playing tricks with my eyes. Wasn't that a small black shape moving away from Maia's hull, about the size of the boat we were in?

"Can you stop rowing for a bit?" I asked.

Barbara stopped and William copied her.

"Not for long," she panted. "We'll get blown backwards. What's the matter?"

"Listen!" I said. "Can't you hear oars?"

We listened.

"It's the water lapping against the flying-boat," William said. But the dog, in the front of the boat with his nose lifted, gave a single, muffled "Woof!"

"*Shut up*, Wat!" Barbara hissed. "Come on, Mouse, we're nearly there."

A few minutes' more hard work by Barbara and William, and we were in the gloom under the giant wing of the flying-boat. William pulled in his oar and grabbed the strut of a float.

"Done it!" William said. But his sister hushed him to silence.

We listened again. The choppy waves flapped against the metal hull. The wind sighed between the struts and the criss-cross rigging. The whole top-heavy shape rocked gently on the water, and the float we were hanging on to plunged up and down. There was no sign of life.

Barbara broke silence.

"Well, Murugan −" she started, but her voice went all hoarse and she had to start again.

"Well, Murugan, we've done our bit. It's up to you now. Lucky you know your way up!"

143

I didn't want to be separated from her, or from my friend Mouse. Even the dog and the leaky boat seemed more friendly than this machine towering above us.

"Come up with me," I said.

"All right, then," she replied.

"Can I come too?" William asked.

"Somebody's got to stay with the dog and the boat," she said firmly.

We pushed the boat across from the float to the side of the hull, and I tried to remember where the handholds were.

"Good-bye, Mugwumps," said Mouse. "Good luck!"

Oh, I wished they could all come with me, all the way.

"Good-bye, Mouse. Thank you for –" I couldn't finish. I had one foot on a step and the other in the boat. I swung over on to the hull.

Barbara was below me, shining her torch. But it had been bad enough climbing up the side of the plane in broad daylight with Harold to help me. Now it felt like climbing a tottering cathedral in the dark. Assisting Barbara made me forget my own fears, a little. Our cold hands clasped as I helped her up on to the wing.

All the time I had kept to myself one fear – or was it a hope? Surely they wouldn't leave two valuable aircraft alone like this, unlocked? It would be silly if we had gone to all this trouble and found ourselves locked out! On the other hand – we could go back to bed then.

But there was an odd knocking sound every time the planes rocked on the water. Barbara shone her torch along the side of Mercury where the sound seemed to come from.

The loading-door of Mercury's hold wasn't even *closed*. It lay a little bit open, bumping against the lock with every roll, just as if – *as if someone had left it like that in a hurry*.

"There!" Barbara breathed. "I told you we could do it! They've even left the door open for us!"

I pulled the door wide open, got up over the sill, and pulled Barbara up after me. Then I knew there was no turning back.

Our feet made clanging echoes in Mercury's hold. We were

out of that chill wind, but the metal walls were icy to touch. Barbara flashed the torch around – and gave a start, grabbing my arm. Dark forms, crouching at the far end of the hold! She kept the beam of light on them steadily.

"Sacks," I whispered.

We went up to them. They were big sacks, some of them quite full, some nearly empty. Each one had a label and a string tied round its throat, and something stencilled on its side: GVIR. I knew what that stood for: King George the Sixth.

"Mail-bags," said Barbara.

I looked at some of the labels: BOMBAY, NEW DELHI, CALCUTTA, MADRAS . . . And for the first time I really believed in this journey I was to make. These names were suddenly more real to me than anything else. They spelt *India*. If those bags were going there, I could too.

"Where's that penknife Mouse gave you?" Barbara asked. I felt in my pocket for the paper bag and the penknife, and handed it to Barbara. What was she going to do with it? I took out the torch too, which I'd forgotten about, and pushed forward the switch. A feeble red glow lit up the bulb and faded out.

"Here, hold mine," Barbara said. The thick strings were sealed with lead seals, and Barbara was cutting the string! The bag was not very full, and the label said MADRAS. She held open the top.

"Get in," she said.

"What do you mean?"

"Get in the bag. Hide there and keep warm. The Royal Mail always gets through."

I couldn't argue with that. I stepped into the bag, trying not to trample too much on the envelopes at the bottom. I gave the torch back to Barbara; she would need it to get down again. She gave me back the penknife. I stood there, holding the mail-bag with my left hand, like a pair of trousers half on and half off.

"Well, good-bye, Mugwumps," she said. I saw her

outstretched hand in the torchlight. I took hold of it and held it for longer than I had ever held it before.

"You will be all right, won't you?" she asked. There was a catch in her voice as if she was trying not to cry. A fine time for *her* to go all soft!

"Come with me," I said. "All the way!"

She hesitated for the briefest of moments.

"I wish I could. But I can't leave Mouse and Wat in the boat."

"I shall be all right," I said. "Thank you for being so kind to me."

"Oh, rot!" she exclaimed, just like her brother. English people don't like good-byes. She dropped my hand and said, "Get right down into that bag. I'll just loop the string round the top. You'll be able to get it open."

I got down into the dusty darkness of the mail-bag, on a cushion of envelopes. Barbara's knee poked into my back as she fastened the string outside – not too tight, I hoped. Then she seemed to be shifting the other sacks around.

"Just piling some more bags round you," I heard her say. Then, "Good-bye, Murugan! Good luck!"

I couldn't reply. I was already a speechless parcel, in the care of His Majesty's Royal Mail. I heard her feet cross the floor, and the door clang shut. She was gone.

And then I could only imagine things in the dark. Was that the sound of a motorboat coming through the water? Did I hear men's voices, and the voices of Barbara and William in reply? Had our plot been discovered, and would they come searching for me? Was I being a coward, lying there snugly while my friends were in trouble? Or would it make it worse for them if I showed myself?

I stayed where I was. No searchers came to look for me. The sounds seemed to fade away. I went back to the sleep I'd been missing since twenty to five that morning. What else was there for me to do?

ALBESON AND THE GERMANS

JAN NEEDLE

Because of the World War II tales told by his grandfather, Albeson hates and fears all Germans. His fears, played on by his destructive friend Smithie, lead him into serious trouble at school and he runs away to sea . . , where he later finds the German sailors are friendly people.

ALBESON RAN for a very long time, until his throat was hot and dry and he was gasping painfully. The rain had stopped sometime during his flight, but he was soaked. It was warm wet, maybe rain, maybe sweat he wasn't sure. He stood in the entrance to a back alley for a while to try and get his breath back. In the light from a dim street lamp he could see steam rising from his clothes.

It was after his lungs had got more or less back to normal that Albeson looked carefully about to see where he'd got to. He recognized the dockland streets near the Camber without surprise. They were totally deserted, not a car or a cat stirring. He listened, raising his head to the breeze. Still quite a loud hum of traffic not far off. It couldn't be the middle of the night then. It was cool and very fresh now, all traces of thunder gone. He sucked in great gouts of clean air, cooling rapidly. It was nice.

Albeson cast around in his mind for what to do next. Smithie had been caught, no doubt of that. There was nothing he could have done to have saved him, so he didn't feel bad about it. You couldn't fight an armed man with a fierce dog and that was that. What would they do to Smithie? How long would it be before he told them Albeson was the other culprit? Would he crack under torture? In any case, thought Albeson, they knew already. His mum and dad would have called the police to look for him by now. He felt a cold hand clutch his heart – what if his father got to him first! He felt like running till he found a policeman and giving himself up. But they'd take him home for starters he supposed, before sending him to jail. Whatever happened he was for it. Ah well, he'd just have to stay away. What else could he do? A midget lorry driver's mate? He snorted. He'd no chance without Smithie, no chance. But what else could he do?

Kicking his toes, thinking gloomy, miserable thoughts, Albeson arrived at the Camber. He turned right onto the quays, wandering round by the gaggle of moored yachts and inshore fishing boats. If Jan the Dutchman's boat was there, with its long overhanging foredeck, he could sleep under that if need be. But the old wooden tub was moored off, alongside a half-built torpedo boat opposite the shipyard. He walked slowly along the coal quay, under the high mobile cranes. Drips of dirty rainwater fell into his hair. Albeson shivered. He was getting dead chilly.

As he turned left at the end of the first quay, he saw that the lights were still on in the 'Bridge'. There was the sound of a lot of men, low but loud. Every now and again a laugh split the air. The benches outside were soaked, so there were no seamen taking the night air with their beer. Albeson was a little surprised. He'd thought it was well after pub time. But then perhaps they didn't care much, down here. As he walked slowly past he looked at the lighted windows. They were misty and he could imagine the warmth inside. That man who'd bought him his crisps and liquid lunch. He drooled at the thought. A packet of crisps. He'd give his left arm . . .

Past the pool of light that spilled onto the puddled

quayside, a black shape loomed into the air. As his eyes got used to the gloom Albeson thought he recognized the high flare of the bows. He went closer. It was the *Carrie*. The white letters, picked out on that proud glistening bow, were as mysterious as ever. But he'd know her anywhere. The *Carrie* from Newcastle.

For a while he forgot the chill, and the hunger, and all the other things. He prowled along in the darkness, keeping close into the wall of the fruit warehouses, studying the lovely lines of his favourite ship.

She was quite still in the black waters of the Camber, with hardly any lights on. The barking of her diesel donkey-engine echoed among the dock buildings as the wind pulled the noise this way and that. Every now and again Albeson got a whiff of fresh diesel oil, then a smell of exhaust fumes. He walked slowly along, from the high bow with its winches, down past the low waist, a jumble of derricks and cables, towards the break of the bridge, that rose flush out of the well-deck to form the poop. The cargo hatches were mainly battened down, just one gaping open. *Carrie* was either about to start unloading, or almost ready to sail.

He couldn't guess how long the ship was, but he took quite a time to get past her. He knew she wasn't big, as ships go. Not like some of the big ones you could see if you stood on the beach with the holiday-makers, the ocean liners and that. Or the supertankers. She wasn't even as big as the Navy ships that filled the harbour. About as long as a submarine, perhaps. But a completely different kettle of fish. He scorned submarines. *Carrie* was beautiful, a real sea-going boat. She'd survive anything, whereas a submarine looked like a tube of toothpaste or a cigar. Built for going under. The *Carrie* was built to ride to the waves, to rise over them and crash down, chucking great gouts of white water out from under her shoulders.

Albeson sat on the wheel of a mobile compressor close by the warehouse and studied her rounded stern. There were lights in the afterhouse, shining across the passageway and

out onto the quay through the big square ports cut in her poop side. But he couldn't see anyone, not even a watchman at the head of the rickety old gangplank tied to her rail. The bridge wings were dark too. No one up there having a quiet smoke and keeping an eye out. Odd that. He'd always assumed that there'd be a watchman. Anyone could sneak on board from what he could see.

It didn't enter Albeson's head that *he* could sneak on board until a steel door in the afterhouse opened and the cook came out. You could tell he was the cook because he was dirty, and small, and built rather like a rat with sandy whiskers. Also he had on a white apron, and his grubby tee shirt was stained with sweat. He walked out of the light and disappeared into another door in the forward part of the afterhouse, under the bridge wing.

Out of the door he'd left wide, poured a smell that nearly killed Albeson. It was hot fat. Hot chip fat. He could practically hear them sizzling and bubbling. The idea came into his mind without him being able to stop it. He dribbled so hard and so suddenly that he had to spit. He wanted worse than he'd ever wanted before. Almost without him knowing it he moved quickly and silently towards the gangway. One fearful glance all round the quay. Still deserted. He crept up the swaying planks.

The noise in the alleyway was much louder than he'd bargained for – the donkey-engine must be close by. He felt afraid, exposed. But the smell streaming from the galley was too much for him. He darted to the doorway and jumped over the steel sill.

Inside it was hot and smoky. The first thing he saw was a sort of range, in shining steel, with two vast open pans on it. They had wire baskets, and golden chips writhed in the boiling fat. Beside the pans were three huge kettles, with steam just starting to push out of their spouts. He glanced about, dribbling down his chin now. On the table a real mountain of bread and marge. Beside the mountain another – of crisp brown chips.

Albeson leapt on the chips as if his life depended on it. He took a great handful and crammed them into his mouth. He almost shrieked. They burnt! He spat them out onto his hand and blew frantically to cool them. He seized a slice of bread and stuffed it in whole. Using both hands he loaded his mouth like a stoker shovelling coal, using the bread to protect it from the hot chips. He glared at the door all the while as though the very strength of his stare could stop the cook from coming back.

It didn't, of course. He'd only swallowed about three mouthfuls – big ones though, that felt like lumps of red-hot barbed wire going down – when he heard the bridge door clang. Ratty was obviously coming back.

When he'd gone up the gangplank into the galley, he'd

hardly been thinking. Certainly the idea of how he'd escape if cornered hadn't entered his starving head. But now Albeson stood petrified. He suddenly realized what he'd done. He couldn't believe it. On top of everything else, to be caught stealing food. From his favourite ship too! It was only seconds before the cook appeared, but in that time Albeson had frozen like a frightened rabbit, looked about like a cornered mouse, and shot through the opposite galley door like a shot from a gun. He hadn't even noticed it when he came in, but there it was, wide open and as welcome as it was unexpected. Ships were wonderful things.

Albeson leaned against the cool steel of the afterhouse, just beside the galley door. He heard the cook enter, whistling between his teeth. He didn't appear to have noticed anything, the whistling never faltered. When Albeson's breath was about back to normal he looked for a way to get off the *Carrie*, to escape back to the quayside.

The alleyway was quite light, so he wanted to get out of it as quickly as possible. The other side of the Camber was only a stone's throw away. If anyone came along for a stroll, or if there was a police or security patrol, he'd be spotted in short order. He could either go forward, towards the bow, or aft. If he went forward he'd have to climb down a ladder to the well deck and cross in front of the bridge to reach the gangplank. If he went aft he'd be in an alleyway all the way round, more or less protected from watching eyes. But if the cook hadn't closed the starboard galley door he'd have to pass it and risk being seen. It was only seconds since Ratty had gone back into his den, but Albeson couldn't remember if he'd heard the steel door close or not.

In the end he went aft, picking his way carefully past the bits of metal that stuck out at all angles in the most unlikely places. He'd never have believed there could have been so much gear lying around, ready to trip you. Once he banged his shin against some mooring bitts and nearly cried out. But he didn't; he wasn't that daft!

All the way round the stern he crept, straining his eyes in

the gloom to make sure he wasn't seen or he didn't bash into things. He was very nervous, panting a bit. His mouth was burnt too. When he stopped to listen and look he sucked at a piece of skin that hung in a long curtain from the top of his mouth. It was sore. Still, his stomach was better. He could almost feel the hot chips and bread lying in it. He was sure he could feel a burnt patch halfway down his chest, inside, where they'd gone down.

The galley door was closed. He could hear the little ratty man whistling away inside. Such a lot of chips and bread. It must be supper time. Albeson wished he could have suppers like that. Tonight especially a supper like that would have gone down a treat. He bet sailors didn't have to worry how much tomato sauce they were allowed.

Almost as soon as he realized it was supper time, Albeson realized he was in trouble. Getting from the quay up the gangway to the galley had taken no time at all; he hadn't even noticed it. But now he was trying to get away the distance was a pretty fair one. He had to creep, to be invisible, to use the shadows. As he reached the break of the poop, as he reached the ladder that led down to the well-deck and the gangplank, he froze like a rabbit once more.

From out of the 'Bridge Tavern' there was pouring a thick mass of men. They were singing loudly and drunkenly, with shouts and laughs thrown in for good measure. Groups were going off in several directions from the main bunch, some to parked cars, others down the road beside the pub or along both branches of the quay. One of the biggest groups, spreading out like a moving inkblot, was heading for the *Carrie*. Straight as a finger it pointed towards the gangway. Even if he ran Albeson would not reach the bottom before the first seaman did.

He stood there for ages. Time had stopped. The first man, a huge black man in a tartan shirt and baggy blue trousers, stepped onto the planks. They sagged and rattled as he climbed up them. He was puffing like a grampus. Albeson turned and fled.

In the dark, in his fear, he forgot the mooring wires and tripped over them. He flew through the air and smashed into the rise of the stern. He cut his mouth open; a fierce burst of pain shot up from his knee all through his body. He clenched his teeth, crying silently, as he crept round the curve of the afterhouse. Once out of sight of the alleyway he half crawled, half scrambled, without the foggiest idea of where he was going. He could hear a jumbled noise as more and more men climbed the steps into the poop alley and made for the galley to get their supper. He couldn't pick out any words at all because he wasn't really listening. He was in terror. If they found him he would die, something terrible would happen. He whimpered and crawled, scrambled and sobbed.

Out of the darkness rose a brown steel thing that was very like a coal scuttle. There was a door in it held closed by a big clip. Albeson bashed at it frantically with his fist. The clip held, his fist hurt as though he'd broken it. Footsteps. Men were coming aft. They'd hang about in the stern, looking over the black water, to eat their chips. They'd get him. He seized the clip with both hands and wrenched with all his might. It slipped down. The metal door swung open.

Albeson scrambled over the sill and almost fell into the black hole. He was very lucky that his leg slipped between the rungs of a vertical ladder and held him. He turned himself the right way up and started to go down the ladder. It was an amazing distance until his feet touched solid plating.

He lay in a heap in the greasy darkness, his blood hammering. He was so thirsty! The door had swung to, but a gleam of light showed round the edges. Where he was, all around him, the blackness was so intense that he could almost feel it. He put his hand in front of his face. But it could not be seen, not even an outline. He had never dreamed that such darkness existed.

Above his head the jumble of noise grew louder. The crew were taking the air as they took their supper. There were clankings and laughter and shouts. Gradually the voices became separate, distinct. Gradually it dawned on Albeson that even when only one voice was going at once he couldn't understand a word that was being said. Gradually it dawned on him that the *Carrie* of Newcastle could not be what she claimed to be. She could not possibly be an English ship. But how? Smithie had read the name dozens of times. Smithie had identified the red black and orange houseflag she wore instead of the Red Ensign.

The thought entered his mind slowly, but he recognized immediately that it was the truth. Smithie could not read either. Nipper, he thought bitterly, you've hit the nail right on the head. Smithie's done you!

A voice above him said something which caused the other men to shout with laughter. Then came a reply. Most of it might have been Greek for all Albeson knew. But the first three words came through as clearly as if they'd been read to him from a page of his comic.

"Donner und Blitzen," said the man, then jabbered on till there was another loud laugh.

The *Carrie* of Newcastle was a German ship.

TSCHIFFELY'S RIDE

A. F. TSCHIFFELY

A. F. Tschiffely got bored with schoolteaching, bought a pair of native South American horses and rode ten thousand miles from Argentina to Washington in the USA. Every page of his account contains an adventure.

LANDSLIDES AND swollen rivers made it impossible to follow the road and compelled me to make a large detour over the mountains to the west. Natives who knew these regions advised me to take a guide, for alone I should have difficulty in finding the direction among the numerous little Indian footpaths.

With the mayor's assistance I found an Indian in a village who agreed to come with me, but unfortunately the man could neither speak nor understand Spanish. I bought some provisions, and without losing time started out, the guide, like most Indians, preferring to go on foot, and even when the horses went at a trot he kept up with us with ease. After some time he led us into very rough country, and often he made a sign to me to go ahead, and then he took a short cut, and later I found him sitting somewhere far ahead, chewing coca whilst waiting for us.

We had crossed some giddy and wobbly hanging bridges before, but here we came to the worst I had ever seen or ever wish to see again. Even without horses the crossing of

158

such bridges is apt to make anybody feel cold ripples running down the back, and, in fact, many people have to be blindfolded and strapped on stretchers to be carried across. Spanning a wild river the bridge looked like a long, thin hammock swung high up from one rock to another. Bits of rope, wire and fibre held the rickety structure together, and the floor was made of sticks laid crosswise and covered with some coarse fibre matting to give a foothold and to prevent slipping that would inevitably prove fatal. The width of this extraordinary piece of engineering was no more than four feet, and its length must have been roughly one hundred and fifty yards. In the middle the thing sagged down like a slack rope.

I went to examine it closely, and the very sight of it made me feel giddy, and the thought of what might easily happen produced a feeling in my stomach as if I had swallowed a block of ice. For a while I hesitated, and then I decided to chance it, for there was no other alternative but to return to Ayacucho and there wait for the dry season. I unsaddled the horses, and giving the Indian the leadline I made signs to him to go ahead with Mancha first. Knowing the horse well, I caught him by the tail and walked behind talking to him to keep him quiet. When we stepped on the bridge he hesitated for a moment, then he sniffed the matting with suspicion, and after examining the strange surroundings he listened to me and cautiously advanced. As we approached the deep sag in the middle, the bridge began to sway horribly, and for a moment I was afraid the horse would try to turn back, which would have been the end of him; but no, he had merely stopped to wait until the swinging motion was less, and then he moved on again. I was nearly choking with excitement, but kept on talking to him and patting his haunches, an attention of which he was very fond. Once we started upwards after having crossed the middle, even the horse seemed to realize that we had passed the worst part, for now he began to hurry towards safety. His weight shook the bridge so much that I had to catch hold of the wires on the sides to keep my balance. Gato, when his turn came, seeing his companion on the other side, gave less trouble and crossed over as steadily as if he were walking along a trail. Once the horses were safely on the other side we carried over the packs and saddles, and when we came to an Indian hut where 'chicha' and other native beverages were sold we had an extra long drink to celebrate our successful crossing, whilst the horses quietly grazed as if they had accomplished nothing out of the way.

From Paramonga north there is a vast desert, close on a hundred miles from one river to the next, and as there is no water to be found there I was obliged to make the crossing in one journey. For this reason I had to wait for the full moon before I could, with a certain degree of safety, attempt this long ride.

I had heard many terrible stories about this sandy wilderness, its very name, 'Matacaballo' (Horse-killer), gave me food for reflection.

After four days' waiting I was ready to start, and as I did not intend to carry water for the horses, I was careful not to give them anything to drink the day before we left, for I wanted them to be thirsty and therefore not likely to refuse a good drink immediately before starting out. For myself I packed two bottles of lemon juice in the saddlebags, and the only food I took with me were a few pieces of chocolate that had been in my pack for some days. Towards evening we were ready, and when the sun was setting we crossed the river, on the other side of which the rolling desert starts. I waited until the horses had finished their drink, and after they had pawed and played with the cool water I mounted, and soon we were on the soft and still hot sands that made a peculiar hissing sound under the hoofs of the animals. The indescribable colours of a tropical sunset were reflected on the glittering waves of the ocean, and the old Indian fortress assumed a tint of gold. Even the inhospitable sandy wastes had changed their dread and desolate appearance, for now the sand dunes and undulations were one mass of colour, from golden brown to dark purple, according to light and shadows. A few belated sea-birds were hurriedly flying towards their distant roosting-places on some rocky island; everything seemed to be different now, except the regular, eternal rolling of the breakers on the shore. No sooner had the last clouds ceased to glow like fading beacon fires than darkness set in, and after a while the moon rose over the mountain ranges in the far east, slowly, majestically; and more than welcome to me.

The sensation of riding on soft sand is a peculiar one at first, until the body becomes used to the peculiar springless

motion of the horse. Knowing that such conditions mean a
great strain on the animal I could not help moving in the
saddle, uselessly endeavouring to assist my mount. We were
twisting and winding our way through among high sand
dunes and, whenever it was possible, I guided the animals
down to the wet sand on the beach where I would urge them
into a slow gallop. Often we came to rocky places or to land-
points which stretched far out, and thus I was forced to make
a detour inland again, frequently for considerable distances.
For the first few hours I observed everything around me and
admired the brilliance of the moon that made the ocean glitter
like silver, and gave the often strange sand formations a
ghostly appearance. Soon even all this became monotonous
to me, and every time I stopped to rest the horses for a while
or to adjust the saddles, I lit a cigarette to help pass the time
away. Shortly before dawn I had to halt for quite a long time,
for the moon had gone down behind some clouds and we
were left in darkness; it would not have been wise to continue
lest I should take the wrong direction or lead the horses into
places where the sand is so soft that they would sink in up to
their bellies.

My instinct for finding the direction had developed to a notable degree by this time, probably because I had not very much to think about besides keeping the horses' noses facing the right way, but even when I knew exactly which way to go, fogs or darkness on several occasions made me think it wiser to wait until I could see.

The first rays of the morning sun were hot, and I rightly anticipated that the day was going to be a 'scorcher'. The horses plodded along as if they realized that they were in the midst of a serious test, and when it was about one hour after noon I noticed that they lifted their heads and sniffed the air. Immediately after they hurried their steps, and I believe they would have broken into a gallop if I had permitted them to do so. I was wondering why the horses were so keen to hurry along, and within an hour I knew the reason, for we arrived at the river, and I am certain that the animals had scented water long before I could see it; obviously Mancha and Gato still possessed the instincts of the wild horse.

Great were my feelings of relief when we left the Matacaballo desert behind us.

*   *   *

The river Santa was the one that gave me most trouble. At the time it was in full flood, and the people thought it would be impossible to swim the horses across the wide, swift river. However, I knew the animals could perform the feat, and as I had no intention of waiting for an indefinite period for it to go down I decided to make the attempt. Natives strongly advised me not to be foolish, for they warned me that the river was very tricky and that if I missed a certain place there was no other chance to land the horses and they would be carried down to the sea.

I heard so many terrible things about the Rio Santa that I went to have a look at it. About half an hour's ride through a veritable jungle, flooded by the waters of the river, brought me to my destination.

I must admit that I did not like the look of things, for not only was the other bank far away, but the mass of water came down with a roar, boiling, seething and tumbling, carrying with it branches and trees, besides which, as some friends who accompanied me explained, there were several rocks just below the surface, and if a horse swam over any of them he would be ripped to pieces. In places where two currents met there were large whirlpools, and it did not take me long to realize that it would be very dangerous to make the attempt unless one happened to be thoroughly acquainted with every detail of the river.

In normal times cattle are swum across by 'chimbadores', who thus earn their living, but when the waters are high nobody ever tries. When we had discussed the question my friends went to look for the best of these men, to ask his opinion. After a long wait he arrived, and having carefully studied the river said that he had his doubts about any animal reaching the other bank, as there was only one possible landing-place, and if this was not reached the horses would be lost. I had been in some bad rivers before, and on every occasion my animals behaved admirably, so I did not hesitate to assure him that they were capable of performing the feat. Finally we arranged to meet next morning and to make the attempt.

The news spread like wildfire among the natives, and next morning a large number of curious people arrived to see the show, some on horses or mules, others on foot. When we reached the proposed scene of action some were already there waiting for us, and even on the rocks on the opposite bank others had taken position.

People cross some of these rivers in a basket slung on a cable, and the one across this river is the longest I have seen, ending on a high rock on the other bank. I unsaddled, and the things were taken across by means of the cable. When I thought everything was ready one of the local authorities, who had been very friendly with me, came up and bluntly told me he would not allow me to enter the river, for such a thing amounted to rank suicide, especially as I did not know the tricks and dangers of these wild waters.

I could already see myself returning a beaten man and waiting for days, or maybe even weeks, before being able to reach that other bank, and just then I saw the 'chimbador' standing near. I offered him a good sum of money if he would swim my animals across, and to this nobody had any objection, for these men are wonderful swimmers and know every inch and trick of the river. At first he refused to consider my offer, but when I agreed that he could leave the horses if he saw that they could not reach the only landing-place and save himself he promised to try.

For a long time he studied the seething river, and sent a few men to different points upstream to signal should branches or trees come floating down. I advised him to mount on Mancha and to leave Gato to follow behind loose. The former would never let anyone but myself ride him on dry land without bucking, so we coaxed him into the water where the man mounted without trouble, and as soon as the 'all clear' signal was given they started to wade out, and in a few moments the current swept the three downstream, Gato following close behind his companion.

The people on the bank had made bets as to whether or not the horses would cross, and I must admit I passed minutes that seemed hours, until at long last there was a loud cheer from many throats and both animals waded out on the other side nearly half a mile downstream. The Rio Santa had been conquered in full flood.

THE DOROBO

ELSPETH HUXLEY

Elspeth was living in Kenya with Kate and Humphrey Crawfurd, and Dirk the helper.

ONE MORNING I surprised two dikdik in the glade, standing among grass that countless quivering cobwebs had silvered all over, each one – and each strand of every cobweb – beaded with dew. It was amazing to think of all the untold millions of cobwebs in all the forest glades, and all across the bush and plains of Africa, and of the number of spiders, more numerous even than the stars, patiently weaving their tents of filament to satisfy their appetites, and of all the even greater millions of flies and bees and butterflies that must go to nourish them; and for what end, no one could say.

In the middle of this field of silver splendour stood two dikdiks with their tiny heads lifted, their nostrils dilated and their unwinking eyes, as bright as blackberries, looking straight into mine. I never ceased to marvel at the delicacy and brittleness of their legs, slender as reeds; it seemed impossible that the dikdiks should not break them as they bounded over tufts or hummocks, even with their leaf-light weight.

These dikdiks had the charm of the miniature. They were perfectly made, not a single hair or sinew less than immaculate; little engines of muscle and grace, more like spirits than creatures. One always saw them in pairs. So long as I stood still, so did the dikdiks; I wondered what would happen if I never moved at all. Would they stand and stare all day? Should we all be there at evening, still motionless? But it was hopeless to try to out-stare the dikdiks; after a while I took a step forward and, with a movement of superb ease and elegance, the little buck sprang away to melt into the trees.

I then became aware, as one so mysteriously does, that I was being watched. I looked round, saw nothing, and stepped forward to sit on a fallen log. A current of watching still trembled in the air. After a while I saw a stirring in the dark undergrowth, and a brown furry figure stepped forth into a shaft of sunlight, which awoke in his fur pelt a rich, rufous glow, and twinkled on his copper ornaments.

He was a small man: not a dwarf exactly, or a pygmy, but one who stood about half-way between a pygmy and an ordinary human. His limbs were light in colour and he wore a cloak of bushbuck skin, a little leather cap, and ear-rings, and carried a long bow and a quiver of arrows. He stood stock-still and looked at me just as the dikdik had done, and I wondered whether he, too, would vanish if I moved.

"*Jambo*," I ventured.

His face crinkled into a smile. It was a different face from that of a Kikuyu, more pointed, lighter-skinned, finer-boned; it wore something of the watchful and defensive look of an animal, with an added humour and repose.

He stepped forward, raised his hand, and returned my greeting.

"The news?" I asked, continuing the traditional form of greeting.

"Good."

"Where have you come from?"

He threw back his head to indicate the hills at his back.

"The forest."

"Where are you going?"

"To seek meat."

He came and stood by me, fingering his bow. We could not speak much, for he knew only about a score of Swahili words. From him came a strong, pungent smell, with a hint of rankness, like a waterbuck's; his skin was well greased with fat, his limbs wiry and without padding, like the dikdiks'. I knew him for a Dorobo, one of that race of hunters living in the forest on game they trapped or shot with poisoned arrows. They did not cultivate, they existed on meat and roots and wild honey, and were the relics of an old, old people who had once had sole possession of these lands – the true aborigines. Then had come others like the Kikuyu and Masai, and the Dorobo had taken refuge in the forests. Now they lived in peace, or at least neutrality, with the herdsmen and cultivators, and sometimes bartered skins and honey for beads, and for spears and knives made by native smiths. They knew all the ways of the forest animals, even of the bongo, the shyest and most beautiful, and their greatest delight was to feast for three days upon a raw elephant.

I knew his arrows would be poisoned. He pulled one out and showed me the sticky black coating on the iron head. "This kills the elephant, the great pig, the buffalo."

"There are many buffaloes?" I asked, thinking of Humphrey's water-furrow, and the warning uttered by the Kikuyu elders.

"Come with me." He turned and walked towards the forest with loping, bent-kneed strides. Where the glade ended the undergrowth looked black and solid as a wall, but he slid into it, and I found that we were on a little path. That was too strong a word for it; it was rather a crack in the spiked solidity where other feet had trodden. The Dorobo stooped, I copied him, and we proceeded slowly like crouching animals, he silently, I treading on sticks and barging into roots and getting caught by creepers and scratched by thorns.

We came to a small glade sloping down towards a stream that could be heard whispering at the bottom, clouded with reeds and long grass. Near the glade's margin was a patch of bare, greyish earth.

"See!" exclaimed the Dorobo, pointing with satisfaction: and I looked in vain for a herd of buffaloes.

"I see nothing."

He loped forward again. When we halted on the edge of the bare patch, I could observe hoof-marks and cattle-droppings; the hint of a rank odour, faintly bovine, hung about the place. It was a salt-lick, tramped by the feet of many buffaloes.

"They come every night," the Dorobo said. "If the bwana brings a gun early in the morning, he will see many, many, just like cattle."

"Where are they now?"

He pointed with his chin to the slopes beyond. "There above. They sleep. They eat salt at night, and in the early morning they play."

We returned along the game-track. "Where is your house?" I asked.

"In the forest."

"You have no shamba?"

"The elephant is my shamba. These are my hoes." He touched the quiver at his side. "Have you tobacco?"

"No." I felt ungrateful, and I had no money either. "I will try to get some."

"Good. Bring it here, and I will take the bwana to the buffaloes." He smiled, half-raised his hand, twitched his bushbuck cloak more securely on his shoulder, and loped off, leaving his ripe civet smell on the morning air.

I wanted to keep the Dorobo to myself, he belonged to the same world as the dikdik and jasmine and butterflies, but I did not know how to get hold of any tobacco; so I was forced to confide in Dirk. His eye gleamed when he heard about the salt-lick.

"That is how to get them, man," he said. "There will be many, big bulls and all. I will find that Kaffir, he will show me the spoor."

"You must take me with you."

Dirk merely laughed. "A *toto* like you?"

"But he's my Dorobo!"

Dirk said that Dorobo belonged to anyone who brought them tobacco, and rode up with some next morning to the furrowhead. Although we had made no appointment, the Dorobo appeared, this time with another, even thinner and smaller than himself. They departed carrying the tobacco, having promised to meet Dirk at the forest's edge next morning, before dawn, and guide him to the lick. As for me, I was to be left out, and resentment stung me like *siafu*. I had discovered the Dorobo, and now Dirk was going to have all the fun.

That night I thumped my head four times on the pillow, so as to wake at four o'clock. Probably it was the stir of Dirk's departure that really woke me, the lanterns moving in the darkness, the tapping on the door of his rondavel, and the pawing and snorting of the pony he was taking as far as the furrowhead, because of his leg. I dressed in the darkness, shivering, for these early mornings were chilly and the water in the jug stung the skin. I waited until the pony had gone and the lights vanished, then I crept out like a vole to follow on foot.

This was not nearly so simple as I had expected. Although a half-moon threw black shadows, the path developed all sorts of bumps, holes, and obstacles unknown in daylight. The grass was soaking wet and bitterly cold, and the twinkling guide-light soon disappeared, leaving me hemmed in by shapes that leant towards me with a crouching menace: leopards, buffaloes, hyenas, even elephants might be within a few feet, gloating at the prospect of a meal. I wished very much that I had stayed in bed, and with every step decided to retreat, but obstinacy drove my reluctant feet forward. Only the furrow hummed a friendly note with its gentle swishing; at least I could not lose the way, so long as I followed it.

As I approached my glade I could hear Dirk's pony cropping grass, and the movement of humans; he and the syce were waiting for the Dorobo. I waited also, frightened to reveal myself, shivering, and getting hungry; a rumbling stomach threatened to betray me, and I wanted to sneeze.

Many hours seemed to pass before the Dorobos' arrival. At last I heard low voices, the jingle of a bridle, an order given, and then silence, save for the noises of the pony, who was to be left behind with the syce while Dirk proceeded, limp and all, on foot.

The syce, a Kikuyu named Karoli, was to some extent an ally, and I decided to ask him to help me follow Dirk into the forest. When I appeared he was at first alarmed, then incredulous, and finally discouraging.

"The bwana told me to stay here," he said. "I do not wish to be eaten by leopards and trampled by buffaloes. Are you not a *toto*? And should not all *totos* be in bed?"

"I shall wait here until he shoots a buffalo."

"It is too cold, and the bwana will be angry."

"I want to stay."

"Haven't you heard about the savage monster that lives in the forest and eats horses? When it smells one, out it comes. It is bigger than a forest pig, it has teeth like swords and five arms like a monkey's, and seven eyes. It will eat you up in one mouthful, like a stork eating a locust."

"You are telling lies."

All the same, I could not help thinking of the monster, with big pointed teeth and burning eyes, and wondering if there might not be a grain of truth in Karoli's tale. I hugged the pony's neck for warmth, convinced by now that bed would, after all, be a much nicer place.

"Why do you not go back to Thika, to your mother and father?" Karoli asked. "Thika is a better place than this. The maize grows tall, and there are sweet potatoes, and the land is fat."

"Is Thika your home, also?"

"Very close to Thika; and Kupanya is the chief of my people. But my family will think I have died in this cold place, for my bwana will not let me go home."

We talked of Thika while the darkness thinned slowly and the stars faded, and the sky glowed with a deep, rich, royal blue. The air was steel-keen, a film of dew lay over everything and a breath of frost passed over the glade, leaving no traces. A rain-bird called; its haunting downward cadence was like a little waterfall, melodious and melancholy.

The gun shot could not now be long delayed. Night was fading so fast that we could see tree-shapes thirty or forty paces distant. Something moved just down the furrow; I watched it fiercely: a leopard on the prowl, a homing forest pig? No, only a bushbuck, his pelt dark with dew, picking his way fastidiously along our glade, his nostrils a-quiver to receive the book of scents from which he could read with certainty the news of the morning.

The crash came and shook the trees: another after it, then a third. These three explosions united to form a hollow echo from the hills, and made the pony plunge and whinny. The sound rolled away into a watchful silence. The bushbuck had vanished, the rain-bird was stilled, only the furrow whispered to itself unchanged. Then from the forest came movement, a muffled crashing, the snap of branches, a thumping of hooves.

"They come towards us," said Karoli.

The sounds were indeed growing louder as the buffaloes, obsessed by panic, stampeded downhill, abandoning all caution in a frantic flight. At such times their big-bossed horns were used like battering-rams to thrust a way through the thickets; in their panic they would plunge ahead with no regard for any object in their way.

"To that tree, quickly!" cried Karoli, tugging at the reins

and trying to pull the pony after him; it smelt the buffaloes, threw up its head, and bolted. I ran to the big cedar where Karoli cowered; he was sweating and rolling his eyes. The buffaloes went by as if a mass of great black boulders had detached themselves from the hillside and come hurtling down upon us at such a speed that they were gone before I had time even to realize what they were; their hoof-beats

made the ground quiver under my feet as if it were a hollow gourd. The boulders vanished, the drumming faded, in a moment only the rank smell remained. Karoli rubbed his head and made chattering sounds. We both sat down on a log to rest our weak knees.

"These buffaloes are bad, bad, bad," said Karoli. "They will crush you with their feet as a man steps upon a beetle. Eee – eee, there were a hundred buffaloes, a thousand, more than the cattle of the Masai; they were angry, they were bad." He went on talking to himself in this vein.

By now the sky in the direction taken by the buffaloes was banded with rose and lemon and the colour of flamingo wings: the path was ready, the sun was on his way. From the forest came three figures led by my Dorobo, whose face was eager as a dog's. Dirk was the last, hampered by his leg. When he saw me he was furious, but had no time for more than swearing; he had wounded a buffalo, and had to find the spoor. Two bulls lay dead near the salt-lick, where he had lain in wait until dawn.

The Dorobo ranged through the glade like hounds casting for a scent, and soon one of them stood rigid and gave a low call. On a leaf-blade was a little crimson bead, which Dirk and the Dorobo bent to examine. By its colour they could tell whether the buffalo had been hit in the body, or in the heart or lungs.

My Dorobo took the lead with his head down and his eyes on the ground, bow in hand. Dirk followed with his rifle. The sun came up proud as a lancer, hurling long golden spears over the dew-white grass and silver cobwebs; a red flame sprang up the trunks of the cedars, the birds fluted, the whole world came alive. Karoli went over to the pool and sluiced his head in the cold upland water.

"Now we must go back with an angry buffalo on the path," he grumbled. "If it sees us it will trample on us, perhaps it is waiting for us now."

Nevertheless we encountered nothing more ferocious than a pair of dikdiks, a distant glimpse of waterbuck, and some francolins. I had entertained a hope of sneaking off to my rondavel unobserved, but this was quickly dispelled. The pony had arrived, and a relief expedition under Mr Crawfurd was about to set forth. He glared at me with an anger all the more alarming for its cold suppression, and told me in icy tones that I deserved to be kept in bed for a week on bread and water. But Kate Crawfurd, although she scolded, was too relieved to be severe, which in any case was not in her nature, and I enjoyed an excellent breakfast, and later in the day went with a party sent to skin and cut up the two dead buffaloes.

Dirk's shots had brought forth from the forest's recesses a little posse of Dorobo who could hardly restrain their excitement as hides were stripped from carcasses to reveal beneath the dark red flesh with its wonderful network of veins and arteries, the viscous blue coiled intestines, the purple liver, and the bright spongy lungs. As the knives sliced away, a murmur of joy and eagerness arose. At a word from the chief skinner they fell upon the raw meat and hacked hunks off with swords and knives, smearing faces and chests with blood and mucus as they dug in their teeth like worrying hounds. The Kikuyu stepped back and looked on with contempt. They ate meat only, as a rule, on ceremonial occasions and, while they relished a fat ram or bullock, they tackled these decorously, old men eating before the young, men before women, each age-grade in its turn.

"They are like hyenas," Karoli said. "If they had no buffaloes or elephants, they would eat men."

But the Dorobo were sublimely happy, immersed in pleasure as a bather in the sea, and holding nothing back. They had no fear, as hyenas must have, of being driven off by stronger creatures; they simply gave way to their appetites, belching to make room for more. After a while their stomachs began to swell up like puffballs, the pace grew slower, and some of them wrapped slabs of meat in leaves to carry home.

Meanwhile, Dirk had not reappeared. Both the Crawfurds

began to get anxious; with a stiff leg he would lack agility, a quality indispensable to trackers of game. Buffaloes were said to double back on their tracks and take their hunter in the rear when they were wounded; a good many people had been killed that way.

"Poor boy, I do hope nothing's happened," Kate Crawfurd exclaimed. "I don't know what I would say to his parents; if it comes to that, I don't know who his parents are, or their address or Christian names or anything; perhaps they haven't got an address but are living in a wagon somewhere, or a laager, whatever that is (apart from a kind of beer); we never ought to have let him go after the buffalo."

"We didn't," Humphrey pointed out.

"Well, that's quite true, though I don't suppose his mother would believe us; perhaps he has just got tired and is coming back very slowly; don't you think we ought to send out a relief expedition, Humphrey, to search for him, with some brandy in case he's hurt, and a stretcher, in case he's quite exhausted?"

"No," Humphrey said.

And he was right: Dirk turned up a few hours later safe and sound, but angry and morose, because the buffalo had eluded him. He and the Dorobo had tracked it for miles, and the buffalo had not doubled back at all but gone very quickly; after a while the blood spoor had petered out.

"It can't be very badly wounded if it's gone so far," Kate said soothingly. "And now you must really go and lie down, Dirk, and rest your leg, goodness knows how you managed to go all that way, I hope you haven't strained it. You mustn't go and hunt buffaloes again until your leg has absolutely recovered."

"The hide was worth at least a hundred and fifty rupees," Dirk grumbled. Humphrey was equally put out to know that a wounded buffalo was at large and might at any moment attack one of his labour force, or indeed attack him.

"The Dorobo will finish it off and gobble it up," Kate Crawfurd said. "How very carnivorous they are! But I suppose we are just as bad, only we cook it first, which makes everything a little more restrained, but doesn't affect the principle, that we all live on dead animals, like hyenas and lions. I used to think that vegetarians were cranks, but now I wonder; perhaps they have climbed a rung higher on the ladder of civilization. Perhaps it is more *spiritual*, to live on beans and spinach, with possibly an egg now and then. Do you think we ought to try it, Humphrey, and give up being carnivores?"

"No."

We ate the buffaloes' liver and enjoyed it, in spite of Kate's doubts; but since then I have often wondered whether she was right.

WHITE FANG

JACK LONDON

Two extracts from the beginning of this famous animal adventure.

DARK SPRUCE FOREST frowned on either side the frozen waterway. The trees had been stripped by a recent wind of their white covering of frost, and they seemed to lean toward each other, black and ominous, in the fading light. A vast silence reigned over the land. The land itself was a desolation, lifeless, without movement, so lone and cold that the spirit of it was not even that of sadness. There was a hint in it of laughter, but of a laughter more terrible than any sadness – a laughter that was mirthless as the smile of the sphinx, a laughter cold as the frost and partaking of the grimness of infallibility. It was the masterful and incommunicable wisdom of eternity laughing at the futility of life and the effort of life. It was the Wild – the savage, frozen-hearted Northland Wild.

But there *was* life, abroad in the land and defiant. Down the frozen waterway toiled a string of wolfish dogs. Their bristly fur was rimed with frost. Their breath froze in the air as it left their mouths, spouting forth in spumes of vapour that settled upon the hair of their bodies and formed into crystals of frost. Leather harness was on the dogs, and leather traces attached them to a sled which dragged along

behind. The sled was without runners. It was made of stout birch-bark, and its full surface rested on the snow. The front end of the sled was turned up, like a scroll, in order to force down and under the bore of soft snow that surged like a wave before it. On the sled, securely lashed, was a long and narrow oblong box. There were other things on the sled – blankets, an axe, and a coffee-pot and frying-pan; but prominent, occupying most of the space, was the long and narrow oblong box.

In advance of the dogs, on wide snowshoes, toiled a man. At the rear of the sled toiled a second man. On the sled, in the box, lay a third man whose toil was over – a man whom the Wild had conquered and beaten down until he would never move nor struggle again. It is not the way of the Wild to like movement. Life is an offence to it, for life is movement; and the Wild aims always to destroy movement.

It freezes the water to prevent it running to the sea; it drives the sap out of the trees till they are frozen to their mighty hearts; and most ferociously and terribly of all does the Wild harry and crush into submission man – man who is the most restless of life, ever in revolt against the dictum that all movement must in the end come to the cessation of movement.

But at front and rear, unawed and indomitable, toiled the two men who were not yet dead. Their bodies were covered with fur and soft tanned leather. Eyelashes and cheeks and lips were so coated with the crystals from their frozen breath that their faces were not discernible. This gave them the seeming of ghostly masques, undertakers in a spectral world at the funeral of some ghost. But under it all they were men, penetrating the land of desolation and mockery and silence, puny adventurers bent on colossal adventure, pitting themselves against the might of a world as remote and alien and pulseless as the abysses of space.

They travelled on without speech, saving their breath for the work of their bodies. On every side was the silence, pressing upon them with a tangible presence. It affected their minds as the many atmospheres of deep water affect the body of the diver. It crushed them with the weight of unending vastness and unalterable decree. It crushed them into the remotest recesses of their own minds, pressing out of them, like juices from the grape, all the false ardours and exaltations and undue self-values of the human soul, until they perceived themselves finite and small, specks and motes, moving with weak cunning and little wisdom amidst the play and inter-play of the great blind elements and forces.

An hour went by, and a second hour. The pale light of the short sunless day was beginning to fade, when a faint cry arose on the still air. It soared upward with a swift rush, till it reached its topmost note, where it persisted, palpitant and tense, and then slowly died away. It might have been a lost soul wailing, had it not been invested with a certain sad fierceness and hungry eagerness. The front man turned his head until his eyes met the eyes of the man behind. And then, across the narrow oblong box, each nodded to the other.

A second cry arose, piercing the silence with needle-like shrillness. Both men located the sound. It was to the rear, somewhere in the snow expanse they had just traversed. A third and answering cry arose, also to the rear and to the left of the second cry.

"They're after us, Bill," said the man at the front.

His voice sounded hoarse and unreal, and he had spoken with apparent effort.

"Meat is scarce," answered his comrade. "I ain't seen a rabbit sign for days."

Thereafter they spoke no more, though their ears were keen for the hunting-cries that continued to rise behind them.

At the fall of darkness they swung the dogs into a cluster of spruce trees on the edge of the waterway, and made a camp. The coffin, at the side of the fire, served for seat and table. The wolf-dogs, clustered on the far side of the fire, snarled and bickered among themselves, but evinced no inclination to stray off into the darkness.

"Seems to me, Henry, they're stayin' remarkable close to camp," Bill commented.

Henry, squatting over the fire and settling the pot of coffee with a piece of ice, nodded. Nor did he speak till he had taken his seat on the coffin and begun to eat.

"They know where their hides is safe," he said. "They'd sooner eat grub than be grub. They're pretty wise, them dogs."

Bill shook his head. "Oh, I don't know."

His comrade looked at him curiously. "First time I ever heard you say anything about their not bein' wise."

"Henry," said the other, munching with deliberation the beans he was eating, "did you happen to notice the way them dogs kicked up when I was a-feedin' 'em?"

"They did cut up more'n usual," Henry acknowledged.

"How many dogs've we got, Henry?"

"Six."

"Well, Henry . . ." Bill stopped for a moment, in order that his words might gain greater significance. "As I was sayin', Henry, we've got six dogs. I took six fish out of the bag. I gave one fish to each dog, an', Henry, I was one fish short."

"You counted wrong."

"We've got six dogs," the other reiterated dispassionately. "I took out six fish. One Ear didn't get no fish. I came back to the bag afterwards an' got 'm his fish."

"We've only got six dogs," Henry said.

"Henry," Bill went on, "I won't say they was all dogs, but there was seven of 'm that got fish."

Henry stopped eating to glance across the fire and count the dogs.

"There's only six now," he said.

"I saw the other one run off across the snow," Bill announced with cool positiveness. "I saw seven."

Henry looked at him commiseratingly and said: "I'll be almighty glad when this trip's over."

"What d' ye mean by that?" Bill demanded.

"I mean that this load of ourn is gettin' on your nerves, an that you're beginnin' to see things."

"I thought of that," Bill answered gravely. "An' so, when I

saw it run off across the snow, I looked in the snow an' saw its tracks. Then I counted the dogs, an' there was still six of 'em. The tracks is there in the snow now. D' ye want to look at 'em? I'll show 'em to you."

Henry did not reply, but munched on in silence, until, the meal finished, he topped it with a final cup of coffee. He wiped his mouth with the back of his hand and said:

"Then you're thinkin' as it was –"

A long wailing cry, fiercely sad, from somewhere in the darkness, had interrupted him. He stopped to listen to it, then he finished his sentence with a wave of his hand toward the sound of the cry, "– one of them?"

Bill nodded. "I'd a blame sight sooner think that than anything else. You noticed yourself the row the dogs made."

Cry after cry, and answering cries, were turning the silence into a bedlam. From every side the cries arose, and the dogs betrayed their fear by huddling together and so close to the fire that their hair was scorched by the heat. Bill threw on more wood, before lighting his pipe.

"I'm thinking you're down in the mouth some," Henry said.

"Henry . . ." He sucked meditatively at his pipe for some time before he went on. "Henry, I was a-thinkin' what a blame sight luckier he is than you an' me'll ever be."

He indicated the third person by a downward thrust of the thumb to the box on which they sat.

"You an' me, Henry, when we die, we'll be lucky if we get enough stones over our carcases to keep the dogs off of us."

"But we ain't got people an' money an' all the rest, like him," Henry rejoined. "Long-distance funerals is somethin' you an' me can't exactly afford."

"What gets me, Henry, is what a chap like this, that's a lord or something in his own country, and that's never had to bother about grub nor blankets – why he comes a-buttin' round the God-forsaken ends of the earth – that's what I can't exactly see."

He might have lived to a ripe old age if he'd stayed to home," Henry agreed.

Bill opened his mouth to speak, but changed his mind. Instead, he pointed toward the wall of darkness that pressed about them from every side. There was no suggestion of form in the utter blackness; only could be seen a pair of eyes gleaming like live coals. Henry indicated with his head a second pair, and a third. A circle of the gleaming eyes had drawn about their camp. Now and again a pair of eyes moved, or disappeared to appear again a moment later.

The unrest of the dogs had been increasing, and they stampeded, in a surge of sudden fear, to the near side of the fire, cringing and crawling about the legs of the men. In the scramble one of the dogs had been overturned on the edge of the fire, and it had yelped with pain and fright as the smell of its singed coat possessed the air. The commotion caused the circle of eyes to shift restlessly for a moment and even to withdraw a bit, but it settled down again as the dogs became quiet.

"Henry, it's a blame misfortune to be out of ammunition."

Bill had finished his pipe and was helping his companion spread the bed of fur and blanket upon the spruce boughs which he had laid over the snow before supper. Henry grunted, and began unlacing his moccasins.

"How many cartridges did you say you had left?" he asked.

"Three," came the answer. "An' I wisht 'twas three hundred. Then I'd show 'em what for, damn 'em!"

He shook his fist angrily at the gleaming eyes, and began securely to prop his moccasins before the fire.

"An' I wisht this cold snap'd break," he went on. "It's ben fifty below for two weeks now. An' I wisht I'd never started on this trip, Henry. I don't like the looks of it. I don't feel right, somehow. An' while I'm wishin', I wisht the trip was over an' done with, an' you an' me a-sittin' by the fire in Fort M'Gurry just about now, an' playin' cribbage – that's what I wisht."

Henry grunted and crawled into bed. As he dozed off he was aroused by his comrade's voice.

"Say, Henry, that other one that come in an' got a fish – why didn't the dogs pitch into it? That's what's botherin' me."

"You're botherin' too much, Bill," came the sleepy response. "You was never like this before. You jes' shut up now, an' to go sleep, an' you'll be all hunkydory in the mornin'. Your stomach's sour – that what's botherin' you."

The men slept, breathing heavily, side by side, under the one covering. The fire died down, and the gleaming eyes drew closer the circle they had flung about the camp. The dogs clustered together in fear, now and again snarling menacingly as a pair of eyes drew close. Once their uproar became so loud that Bill woke up. He got out of bed carefully, so as not to disturb the sleep of his comrade, and threw more wood on the fire. As it began to flame up, the circle of eyes drew farther back. He glanced casually at the huddling dogs. He rubbed his eyes and looked at them more sharply. Then he crawled back into the blankets.

"Henry," he said. "Oh, Henry!"

Henry groaned as he passed from sleep to waking, and demanded: "What's wrong now?"

"Nothin'," came the answer; "only there's seven of 'em again. I just counted."

Henry acknowledged receipt of the information with a grunt that slid into a snore as he drifted back into sleep.

In the morning it was Henry who awoke first and routed his companion out of bed. Daylight was yet three hours away, though it was already six o'clock; and in the darkness Henry went about preparing breakfast, while Bill rolled the blankets and made the sled ready for lashing.

"Say, Henry," he asked suddenly, "how many dogs did you say we had?"

"Six."

"Wrong," Bill proclaimed triumphantly.

"Seven again?" Henry queried.

"No, five; one's gone."

"The hell!" Henry cried in wrath, leaving the cooking to come and count the dogs.

"You're right, Bill," he concluded. "Fatty's gone."

"An' he went like greased lightnin' once he got started. Couldn't 've seen 'm for smoke."

"No chance at all," Henry concluded. "They jus' swallowed'm alive. I bet he was yelpin' as he went down their throats, damn 'em!"

"He always was a fool dog," said Bill.

"But no fool dog ought to be fool enough to go off an' commit suicide that way." He looked over the remainder of the team with a speculative eye that summed up instantly the salient traits of each animal. "I bet none of the others would do it."

"Couldn't drive 'em away from the fire with a club," Bill agreed. "I always did think there was somethin' wrong with Fatty anyway."

And this was the epitaph of a dead dog on the Northland trail – less scant than the epitaph of many another dog, of many a man.

(Despite all that Henry and Bill can do to stop her, the 'seventh dog', a mysterious she-wolf, lures the dog team one by one to be food for the wolf pack.)

The day began auspiciously. They had lost no dogs during the night, and they swung out upon the trail and into the silence, the darkness, and the cold with spirits that were fairly light. Bill seemed to have forgotten his forebodings of the previous night, and even waxed facetious with the dogs when, at midday, they overturned the sled on a bad piece of trail.

It was an awkward mix-up. The sled was upside-down and jammed between a tree-trunk and a huge rock, and they were forced to unharness the dogs in order to straighten out the tangle. The two men were bent over the sled and trying to right it, when Henry observed One Ear sidling away.

"Here, you, One Ear!" he cried, straightening up and turning around on the dog.

But One Ear broke into a run across the snow, his traces trailing behind him. And there, out in the snow of their back track, was the she-wolf waiting for him. As he neared her, he became suddenly cautious. He slowed down to an alert and mincing walk and then stopped. He regarded her carefully and dubiously, yet desirefully. She seemed to smile at him, showing her teeth in an ingratiating rather than a menacing way. She moved toward him a few steps, playfully, and then halted. One Ear drew near to her, still alert and cautious, his tail and ears in the air, his head held high.

He tried to sniff noses with her, but she retreated playfully and coyly. Every advance on his part was accompanied by a corresponding retreat on her part. Step by step she was alluring him away from the security of his human companionship. Once, as though a warning had in vague ways flitted through his intelligence, he turned his head and looked back at the overturned sled, at his team-mates, and at the two men who were calling to him.

But whatever idea was forming in his mind was dissipated by the she-wolf, who advanced upon him, sniffed noses with him for a fleeting instant, and then resumed her coy retreat before his renewed advances.

In the meantime, Bill had bethought himself of the rifle. But it was jammed beneath the overturned sled, and by the time Henry had helped him to right the load One Ear and the she-wolf were too close together and the distance too great to risk a shot.

Too late, One Ear learned his mistake. Before they saw the cause, the two men saw him turn and start to run back toward them. Then, approaching at right angles to the trail and cutting off his retreat, they saw a dozen wolves, lean and grey, bounding across the snow. On the instant, the she-wolf's coyness and playfulness disappeared. With a snarl she sprang upon One Ear. He thrust her off with his shoulder, and, his retreat cut off and still intent on regaining the sled, he altered his course in an attempt to circle around to it. More wolves were appearing every moment and joining in the chase. The she-wolf was one leap behind One Ear and holding her own.

"Where are you goin'?" Henry suddenly demanded, laying his hand on his partner's arm.

Bill shook it off. "I won't stand it," he said. "They ain't a-goin' to get any more of our dogs if I can help it."

Gun in hand, he plunged into the underbrush that lined the side of the trail. His intention was apparent enough. Taking the sled as the centre of the circle that One Ear was making, Bill planned to tap that circle at a point in advance of the pursuit. With his rifle, in the broad daylight, it might be possible for him to awe the wolves and save the dog.

"Say, Bill!" Henry called after him. "Be careful! Don't take no chances!"

Henry sat down on the sled and watched. There was nothing else for him to do. Bill had already gone from sight; but now and again, appearing and disappearing amongst the underbrush and the scattered clumps of spruce, could be seen One Ear. Henry judged his case to be hopeless. The dog was thoroughly alive to its danger, but it was running on the outer circle while the wolf-pack was running on the inner and shorter circle. It was vain to think of One Ear so outdistancing his pursuers as to be able to cut across their circle in advance of them and to regain the sled.

The different lines were rapidly approaching a point. Somewhere out there in the snow, screened from his sight by trees and thickets, Henry knew that the wolf-pack, One Ear, and Bill were coming together. All too quickly, far more quickly than he had expected, it happened. He heard a shot, then two shots in rapid succession, and he knew that Bill's ammunition was gone. Then he heard a great outcry of snarls and yelps. He recognized One Ear's yell of pain and terror, and he heard a wolf-cry that bespoke a stricken animal. And that was all. The snarls ceased. The yelping died away. Silence settled down again over the lonely land.

He sat for a long while upon the sled. There was no need for him to go and see what had happened. He knew it as though it had taken place before his eyes. Once he roused with a start and hastily got the axe out from underneath the lashings. But for some time longer he sat and brooded, the two remaining dogs crouching and trembling at his feet.

At last he arose in a weary manner, as though all the resilience had gone out of his body, and proceeded to fasten the dogs to the sled. He passed a rope over his shoulder, a man-trace, and pulled with the dogs. He did not go far. At the first hint of darkness he hastened to make a camp, and he saw to it that he had a generous supply of firewood. He fed the dogs, cooked and ate his supper, and made his bed close to the fire.

But he was not destined to enjoy that bed. Before his eyes closed the wolves had drawn too near for safety. It no longer required an effort of the vision to see them. They were all about him and the fire, in a narrow circle, and he could see them plainly in the firelight, lying down, sitting up, crawling forward on their bellies, or slinking back and forth. They even slept. Here and there he could see one curled up in the snow like a dog, taking the sleep that was now denied himself.

He kept the fire brightly blazing, for he knew that it alone intervened between the flesh of his body and their angry fangs. His two dogs stayed close by him, one on either side, leaning against him for protection, crying and whimpering, and at times snarling desperately when a wolf approached a little closer than usual. At such moments, when his dogs snarled, the whole circle would be agitated, the wolves coming to their feet and pressing tentatively forward, a chorus of snarls and eager yelps rising about him. Then the circle would lie down again, and here and there a wolf would resume its broken nap.

But this circle had a continuous tendency to draw in upon him. Bit by bit, an inch at a time, with here a wolf bellying forward, and there a wolf bellying forward, the circle would narrow until the brutes were almost within springing distance. Then he would seize brands from the fire and hurl them into the pack. A hasty drawing back always resulted, accompanied by angry yelps and frightened snarls when a well-aimed brand struck and scorched a too-daring animal.

Morning found the man haggard and worn, wide-eyed from want of sleep. He cooked breakfast in the darkness, and at nine o'clock, when, with the coming of daylight, the wolf-pack drew back, he set about the task he had planned through the long hours of the night. Chopping down young saplings, he made them crossbars of a scaffold by lashing them high up to the trunks of standing trees. Using the sled-lashing for a heaving rope, and with the aid of the dogs, he hoisted the coffin to the top of the scaffold.

"They got Bill, an' they may get me, but they'll sure never get you, young man," he said, addressing the dead body in its tree sepulchre.

Then he took the trail, the lightened sled bounding along behind the willing dogs; for they, too, knew that safety lay open in the gaining of Fort M'Gurry. The wolves were now more open in their pursuit, trotting sedately behind and ranging along on either side, their red tongues lolling out, their lean sides showing the undulating ribs with every movement. They were very lean, mere skin-bags stretched over bony

frames, with strings for muscles – so lean that Henry found it in his mind to marvel that they still kept their feet and did not collapse forthright in the snow.

He did not dare travel until dark. At midday, not only did the sun warm the southern horizon, but it even thrust its upper rim, pale and golden, above the skyline. He received it as a sign. The days were growing longer. The sun was returning. But scarcely had the cheer of its light departed, than he went into camp. There were still several hours of grey daylight and sombre twilight, and he utilized them in chopping an enormous supply of firewood.

With night came horror. Not only were the starving wolves growing bolder, but lack of sleep was telling upon Henry. He dozed despite himself, crouching by the fire, the blankets about his shoulders, the axe between his knees, and on either side a dog pressing close against him. He awoke once and saw in front of him, not a dozen feet away, a big grey wolf, one of the largest of the pack. And even as he looked, the brute deliberately stretched himself after the manner of a lazy dog, yawning full in his face and looking upon him with a possessive eye, as if, in truth, he were merely a delayed meal that was soon to be eaten.

This certitude was shown by the whole pack. Fully a score he could count, staring hungrily at him or calmly sleeping in the snow. They reminded him of children gathered about a spread table and awaiting permission to begin to eat. And he was the food they were to eat! He wondered how and when the meal would begin.

As he piled wood on the fire he discovered an appreciation of his own body which he had never felt before. He watched his moving muscles and was interested in the cunning mechanism of his fingers. By the light of the fire he crooked his fingers slowly and repeatedly, now one at a time, now all together, spreading them wide or making quick, gripping movements. He studied the nail-formation, and prodded the finger-tips, now sharply, and again softly, gauging the while the nerve-sensations produced. It fascinated him, and he grew suddenly fond of this subtle flesh of his that worked so beautifully and smoothly and delicately. Then he would cast a glance of fear at the wolf-circle drawn expectantly about him, and like a blow the realization would strike him that this wonderful body of his, this living flesh, was no more than so much meat, a quest of ravenous animals, to be torn and slashed by their hungry fangs, to be sustenance to them as the moose and the rabbit had often been sustenance to him.

He came out of a doze that was half nightmare to see the red-hued she-wolf before him. She was not more than half a dozen feet away, sitting in the snow and wistfully regarding him. The two dogs were whimpering and snarling at his feet, but she took no notice of them. She was looking at the man, and for some time he returned her look. There was nothing threatening about her. She looked at him merely with a great wistfulness, but he knew it to be the wistfulness of an equally great hunger. He was the food, and the sight of him excited in her the gustatory sensations. Her mouth opened, the saliva drooled forth, and she licked her chops with the pleasure of anticipation.

A spasm of fear went through him. He reached hastily for a brand to throw at her. But even as he reached, and before his fingers had closed on the missile, she sprang back into safety; and he knew that she was used to having things

thrown at her. She had snarled as she sprang away, baring her white fangs to their roots, all her wistfulness vanishing, being replaced by a carnivorous malignity that made him shudder. He glanced at the hand that held the brand, noticing the cunning delicacy of the fingers that gripped it, how they adjusted themselves to all the inequalities of the surface, curling over and under and about the rough wood, and one little finger, too close to the burning portion of the brand, sensitively and automatically writhing back from the hurtful heat to a cooler gripping-place; and in the same instant he seemed to see a vision of those same sensitive and delicate fingers being crushed and torn by the white teeth of the she-wolf. Never had he been so fond of this body of his as now when his tenure of it was so precarious.

All night, with burning brands, he fought off the hungry pack. When he dozed, despite himself, the whimpering and snarling of the dogs aroused him. Morning came, but for the first time the light of day failed to scatter the wolves. The man waited in vain for them to go. They remained in a circle about him and his fire, displaying an arrogance of possession that shook his courage born of the morning light.

He made one desperate attempt to pull out on the trail. But the moment he left the protection of the fire, the boldest wolf leaped for him, but leaped short. He saved himself by springing back, the jaws snapping together a scant six inches from his thigh. The rest of the pack was now up and surging upon him, and a throwing of firebrands right and left was necessary to drive them back to a respectful distance.

Even in the daylight he did not dare to leave the fire to chop fresh wood. Twenty feet away towered a huge dead spruce. He spent half the day extending his camp-fire to the tree, at any moment a half-dozen burning faggots ready at hand to fling at his enemies. Once at the tree, he studied the surrounding forest in order to fell the tree in the direction of the most firewood.

The night was a repetition of the night before, save that the need for sleep was becoming overpowering. The snarling of his dogs was losing its efficacy. Besides, they were snarling all the time, and his benumbed and drowsy senses no longer took note of changing pitch and intensity. He awoke with a start. The she-wolf was less than a yard from him. Mechanically, at short range, without letting go of it, he thrust a brand full into her open and snarling mouth. She sprang away, yelling with pain, and while he took delight in the smell of burning flesh and hair, he watched her shaking her head and growling wrathfully a score of feet away.

But this time, before he dozed again, he tied a burning pine-knot to his right hand. His eyes were closed but few minutes when the burn of the flame on his flesh awakened him. For several hours he adhered to this programme. Every time he was thus awakened he drove back the wolves with

flying brands, replenished the fire, and rearranged the pine-knot on his hand. All worked well, but there came a time when he fastened the pine-knot insecurely. As his eyes closed it fell away from his hand.

He dreamed. It seemed to him that he was in Fort M'Gurry. It was warm and comfortable, and he was playing cribbage with the Factor. Also, it seemed to him that the fort was besieged by wolves. They were howling at the very gates, and sometimes he and the Factor paused from the game to listen and laugh at the futile efforts of the wolves to get in. And then, so strange was the dream, there was a crash. The door was burst open. He could see the wolves flooding into the big living-room of the fort. They were leaping straight for him and the Factor. With the bursting open of the door, the noise of their howling had increased tremendously. This howling now bothered him. His dream was merging into something else he knew not what; but through it all, following him, persisted the howling.

And then he awoke to find the howling real. There was a great snarling and yelping. The wolves were rushing him. They were all about him and upon him. The teeth of one had closed upon his arm. Instinctively he leaped into the fire, and as he leaped he felt the sharp slash of teeth that tore through the flesh of his leg. Then began a fire fight. His stout mittens temporarily protected his hands, and he scooped live coals into the air in all directions, until the camp-fire took on the semblance of a volcano.

But it could not last long. His face was blistering in the heat, his eyebrows and lashes were singed off, and the heat was becoming unbearable to his feet. With a flaming brand in each hand, he sprang to the edge of the fire. The wolves had been driven back. On every side, wherever the live coals had fallen, the snow was sizzling, and every little while a retiring wolf, with wild leap and snort and snarl, announced that one such live coal had been stepped upon.

Flinging his brands at the nearest of his enemies, the man thrust his smouldering mittens into the snow and stamped about to cool his feet. His two dogs were missing, and he well knew that they had served as a course in the protracted meal which had begun days before with Fatty, the last course of which would likely be himself in the days to follow.

"You ain't got me yet!" he cried, savagely shaking his fist at the hungry beasts; and at the sound of his voice the whole circle was agitated, there was a general snarl, and the she-wolf slid up close to him across the snow and watched him with hungry wistfulness.

He set to work to carry out a new idea that had come to him. He extended the fire into a large circle. Inside this circle he crouched, his sleeping outfit under him as a protection against the melting snow. When he had thus disappeared

within his shelter of flame, the whole pack came curiously to the rim of the fire to see what had become of him. Hitherto they had been denied access to the fire, and they now settled down in a close-drawn circle, like so many dogs, blinking and yawning and stretching their lean bodies in the unaccustomed warmth. Then the she-wolf sat down, pointed her nose at a star, and began to howl. One by one the wolves joined her, till the whole pack, on haunches, with noses pointed skyward, was howling its hungry-cry.

Dawn came, and daylight. The fire was burning low. The fuel had run out, and there was need to get more. The man attempted to step out of his circle of flame, but the wolves surged to meet him. Burning brands made them spring aside, but they no longer sprang back. In vain he strove to drive them back. As he gave up and stumbled inside his circle, a wolf leaped for him, missed, and landed with all four feet in the coals. It cried out with terror, at the same time snarling, and scrambled back to cool its paws in the snow.

The man sat down on his blankets in a crouching position. His body leaned forward from his hips. His shoulders, relaxed and drooping, and his head on his knees advertised that he had given up the struggle. Now and again he raised his head to note the dying down of the fire. The circle of flame and coals was breaking into segments with openings in between. These openings grew in size, the segments diminished.

"I guess you can come an' get me any time," he mumbled. "Anyway, I'm goin' to sleep."

Once he wakened, and in an opening in the circle, directly in front of him, he saw the she-wolf gazing at him.

Again he awakened, a little later, though it seemed hours to him. A mysterious change had taken place – so mysterious a change that he was shocked wider awake. Something had happened. He could not understand at first. Then he discovered it. The wolves were gone. Remained only the trampled snow to show how closely they had pressed him.

Sleep was welling up and gripping him again, his head was sinking down upon his knees, when he roused with a sudden start.

There were cries of men, the churn of sleds, the creaking of harnesses, and the eager whimpering of straining dogs. Four sleds pulled in from the river bed to the camp among the trees. Half a dozen men were about the man who crouched in the centre of the dying fire. They were shaking and prodding him into consciousness. He looked at them like a drunken man and maundered in strange, sleepy speech:

"Red she-wolf . . . Come in with the dogs at feedin' time . . . First she ate the dog-food . . . Then she ate the dogs . . . An' after that she ate Bill . . ."

"Where's Lord Alfred?" one of the men bellowed in his ear, shaking him roughly.

He shook his head slowly. "No, she didn't eat him . . . He's roostin' in a tree at the last camp."

"Dead?" the man shouted.

"An' in a box," Henry answered. He jerked his shoulder petulantly away from the grip of his questioner. "Say, you lemme alone . . . I'm jes' plump tuckered out . . . Goo' night, everybody."

His eyes fluttered and went shut. His chin fell forward on his chest. And even as they eased him down upon the blankets his snores were rising on the frosty air.

But there was another sound. Far and faint it was, in the remote distance, the cry of the hungry wolf-pack as it took the trail of other meat than the man it had just missed.

LEOPARD HUNT

PRINCE MODUPE

WHEN LIGHT flooded the tops of the trees, Lamina's hand pressed heavily on my shoulder. He was looking at me but saying nothing. I wanted him to say something. I wondered whether he would camp on the spot and wait for me to emerge from the forest. Or would he go back to the village? I hoped he would wait but I did not want to ask him to do it. Lamina's hand pressed deeper into my shoulder. He felt my muscles, nodded his head in approval. He redipped my arrows and the tip of my *fange* sword into the poison. I was armed with all any man should need.

I passed through the clinging screen of matted creepers ahead of the daylight. The enormous boles of the tree trunks were only a little darker than the spaces between them. I thought about leopards, hoping the power of my thought would bring one to me. This was the hour when they look for resting places after a night of prowling and killing. Often the rest place is a cave. But I knew of no such cave in this forest, only that the whole jungle seemed an enormous cave, roofed with darkness. The smell of the forest was cave-damp. Under my bare feet was moss. I longed for dry brittle things – twigs snapping in the fire of my mother's kitchen, a grass sleeping mat under my body, thatch rustling on a roof above my head.

201

I stood quietly on the moss, trying to let myself be filled with the feel of the forest. I had food with me for three days, but I hoped I would not have to stay that long. My stomach could hold out for three sundowns but I was not sure about my courage. A leopard who finds himself at daybreak some distance from his lair usually takes his day's rest on a tree limb. This gives him a lookout position from which he can pounce on anyone or anything passing below. Many leopards lived in this jungle; we had the pelts of many who had died in this bush. I felt that death might be waiting for me above my head in any tree.

I pressed on deeper into the forest along a narrow trail, making silent talk of encouragement to myself. My eyes ached with the great effort of trying to watch for danger above me, all around me. Part of the terror was that of being alone. Africans conduct most of their activities in groups. We are not a solitary people. Our strength is in our togetherness.

After a while the thought came to me that instead of walking about aimlessly and exposing myself to the unseen, I would do better to find the evening watering place of the forest animals and conceal myself.

I felt better as soon as I had decided to become the hidden aggressor myself instead of waiting for death to drop down upon me from every overhanging limb. I made myself interested in the slope of the land, such slope as there was. I was still wary but I was over the paralysis of sheer panic. Not every twisted liana was a python waiting to crush me in its coils. Not every rustle hidden by trees was a devourer. I found a small ravine and worked my way down its slopes.

The ravine ended as I hoped it would in a small clear stream cutting through the forest. The relief of seeing bright sunlight sparkling on water was exhilarating after the massed gloom of the forest. The very odour of the jungle is the odour of death – the rotting vegetation, the sickish sweet masses of fungi, the overhanging perfume of blossom on vines which have worked their way up above the crown of

the trees. The thump of a falling seed pod is loud as a crack of thunder in this vast silence. The mass of the growth, the extravagance of vegetation belittles man, shrinks him to grub size. That is perhaps the real terror of jungle, more frightening than the tooth and claw hazards, although they, too, are awesome.

Along the bank of the stream I found a shelter which had been formed in flood stage, an undercut bank. In it I was protected from above, behind, and beneath me. I could at least see what approached, if any danger stalked me.

In the clay where an animal run entered the stream, I saw that the feet of many animals had brought them here to drink. Much as I wanted to see the tracks to know what animals had made them, I resisted because there must be no man-smell to keep them away at dusk. I tested the wind with a clod, crumbled to dust. I was downwind from the watering hole.

It was past midday when I had located my waiting spot. Not too long to wait before the silent forest would come alive. I began to notice details around me. A fallen giant of a tree lay out over the water and a great mass of debris had lodged in the branches. A red and blue lizard whose skin was bright as beads slithered over the trunk. I lost sight of him but soon a great monitor lizard as long as I was tall crept into sight, then lay absolutely quiet, waiting, as I thought, for a waterfowl to perch within his reach. He was screened from above by the foliage of a still-green branch, and from where I sat he seemed nothing more than a sun-dappled swelling on the trunk. He must have seemed nothing more than that to the red-footed webbed creature who became his victim. A whole pageant of small animal life passed before me during the afternoon. Strange as it may seem, I even dozed a few minutes. The heat was relaxing and I felt reasonably secure. My one great fear was not of the animal I hoped to get at evening, but that I would have to spend the night alone in this spot.

I know now that the terrible sounds which come out of the jungle at night are made by animals, creatures like the tree hyraxes and pottos, but even our cleverest hunters believed that the unearthly, skin-chilling night sounds of the forest were made by malevolent spirits. There is no hiding place against demons, the nightmarish creatures of imagination. As for the actual, the four-footed dangers, even a hyena is brave at night. There was a considerable growth of reeds along the banks of the stream and this I saw as a good sign for my purposes. It was the kind of growth where a leopard would skulk waiting for game to pass. I began to think of the leopard I hoped to see as a sort of release from the horror of having to spend the night by the river.

The first large creatures I saw at the water hole were a pair of red river hogs. They were so close to me I could see the coarse texture of their bright red-orange bristles, the white tufts at the ends of the ears. They drank, muddied the water, passed on to the other side of the stream. No rustle in the reeds as yet.

A little water chevrotan drank daintily a bit upstream from the hogs and took to the water keeping only his nose above the surface. He would have been easy prey for a waiting leopard, I thought, but there was scarcely a breeze-ripple in the reeds. Monkeys, little grey colobus creatures, swung out on branches overhanging the water. There was a great troop of them and they seemed to be having a nasty family palaver of some sort which none of them could settle.

Fruit-eating bats darted in and around the monkeys making weird cries from their monstrous fleshy lips.

I saw none of the omen-birds, no sign was given me of what I might expect at any moment.

I watched a number of antelope nuzzling the water, shaking their heads, drinking, ears alert. There were several fawns in the group which the adults kept screened with their own bodies. They sensed lurking danger before I did, gave me the cue to tauten my bow. I could not get to my knees in the cramped spot I was in. Slowly, I eased forward; slowly, a bit at a time, changed from my left to my right knee. I could feel the satisfying flex of the bow in my hand. Not out of the reeds as I had expected, but on the bank above the watering place, and to my right, the head and part profile of a large leopard came into view. He was watching the antelope, which gave me time for careful aim. I let go the arrow with all the force I could muster.

There followed a great commotion, a blood-curdling growl, as the beast leaped toward me. He seemed to come toward me with the same whiz of speed that my own arrow had taken toward him.

I cannot remember side-stepping that straight yellow streak or reaching for my *fange* sword, or crouching for combat. Yet I must have done all of these things. I do remember that the leopard peeled back his lips, that the bared teeth clicked like gourd shake-shakes, and that its breath was foul. I gathered all my strength behind the plunge of my poisoned *fange* but the brute's claws found me. Blinded by a shower of my own blood streaming down from my scalp, I did not see the paw stroke which knocked the *fange* from my hand. My 'one claw' was gone!

Somehow my hands found the animal's throat. The poison on my weapons was taking heavy toll of the beast's strength.

I knew I had only to keep my hands pressed on its throat and his claws out of my belly until the poison had finished its work. The animal, even after its eyes began to dim, seemed capable of twisting and turning over inside its fur. My strength was going, too. My legs had been clawed and I slid around in my own blood as I tried to clamp my knees against its ribs. My thumbs gouged into the neck fur where I thought the windpipe should be.

When I felt I could not hold on another moment, I sensed Lamina at my side. Lamina's presence was so real to me that the numbness in my shoulders seemed to be his hand pressing strength into me. Then my senses clouded and I did not feel Lamina's nearness any more.

When I regained consciousness, I was not in the forest, I was in my mother's house. A great many people were doing a great many things. I could not distinguish one person from another. It was like seeing, from a great distance, boulders which might or might not be elephants. Slowly, I sorted them out. The *Alamami* was there crushing tree barks, squeezing berries, bruising leaves. Several lesser medicine men were helping him. The odours of these forest things carried me back to the jungle and my eyes hurt.

I floated through empty space again until the medicine man began pressing my wounds open, making the clawed places gape like mouths to receive the medicines which were being poured into them. I realized dimly through the pain what they were doing. *A leopard kills after he is dead*. This is a bush saying which means that even if a man survives a mauling he is likely to die from infection in the claw wounds.

They bandaged me with leaves and made me drink broths. When they thought I was strong enough to face the sight, they let me look at the calf of my leg. The medicine man told me I would walk again but I did not see how it would be possible. Too much of me was missing. Yet before the moon had filled twice, I was able to hobble over to Lamina's house and sit in the sun with him.

I felt an awkward shyness about speech with Lamina. I

knew that I was supposed to speak with him as a fellow hunter, a brother. All of my training had been to regard him as a reverenced master. A certain pride, not to be confused with arrogance, was supposed to be in me now. This was too new to sit on me easily. I was quite sure that it was Lamina who had carried me out of the forest, yet no one would tell me that it was. I wanted to find out but I did not know the proper way to ask. I started by feeling around the edges of the subject. Had Lamina camped at the place where he gave me good-by?

He told me then how he had gone to bed early as was his custom but had not been able to sleep. His heart had beat like a message drum. He had sat up in bed wondering what to do. He had heard the bird of evil omen cry three times, long and wailing. He had risen and collected his weapons. Only then did the bird cease lamenting.

When Lamina was mounted on his horse and headed in the direction of the forest, he said that it seemed to him that the beat of his heart was with that of the earth, so he knew he was doing the right thing.

It was dawn by the time Lamina had found me and bound my wounds with herbs and leaves. He had managed to get me across the horse's back and bring me home, no easy matter since the leopard's blood smell was on me. Afterward, he had gone back to skin the dead leopard.

I was worried about whether I would ever walk right again. A lame man is of little use to his tribe. Lamina was sure that I would. He was right. I have no limp but I bear the scars of the leopard's claws on my left leg.

THE LEOPARD

RUSKIN BOND

I FIRST SAW the leopard when I was crossing the small stream at the bottom of the hill.

The ravine was so deep that for most of the day it remained in shadow. This encouraged many birds and animals to emerge from cover during daylight hours. Few people ever passed that way: only milkmen and charcoal-burners from the surrounding villages.

As a result, the ravine had become a little haven of wildlife, one of the few natural sanctuaries left near Mussoorie, a hill station in northern India.

Below my cottage was a forest of oak and maple and Himalayan rhododendron. A narrow path twisted its way down through the trees, over an open ridge where red sorrel grew wild, and then steeply down through a tangle of wild raspberries, creeping vines and slender bamboo.

At the bottom of the hill the path led on to a grassy verge, surrounded by wild dog roses. (It is surprising how closely the flora of the lower Himalayas, between 5,000 to 8,000 feet, resembles that of the English countryside.)

The stream ran close by the verge, tumbling over smooth pebbles, over rocks worn yellow with age, on its way to the plains and to the little Song River and finally to the sacred Ganges.

When I first discovered the stream it was early April and

the wild roses were flowering – small white blossoms lying in clusters.

I walked down to the stream almost every day, after two or three hours of writing. I had lived in cities too long, and had returned to the hills to renew myself, both physically and mentally. Once you have lived with mountains for any length of time, you belong to them, and must return again and again.

Nearly every morning, and sometimes during the day, I heard the cry of the barking deer. And in the evening, walking through the forest, I disturbed parties of pheasant. The birds went gliding down the ravine on open, motionless wings. I saw pine martens and a handsome red fox, and I recognized the footprints of a bear.

As I had not come to take anything from the forest, the birds and animals soon grew accustomed to my presence; or possibly they recognized my footsteps. After some time, my approach did not disturb them.

The langurs in the oak and rhododendron trees, who would at first go leaping through the branches at my approach, now watched me with some curiosity as they munched the tender green shoots of the oak.

The young ones scuffled and wrestled like boys, while their parents groomed each other's coats, stretching themselves out on the sunlit hillside. But one evening, as I passed, I heard them chattering in the trees, and I knew I was not the cause of their excitement.

As I crossed the stream and began climbing the hill, the grunting and chattering increased, as though the langurs were trying to warn me of some hidden danger. A shower of pebbles came rattling down the steep hillside, and I looked up to see a sinewy, orange-gold leopard poised on a rock about 20 feet above me.

It was not looking toward me, but had its head thrust attentively forward, in the direction of the ravine. Yet it must have sensed my presence, because it slowly turned its head and looked down at me.

It seemed a little puzzled at my presence there; and when, to give myself courage, I clapped my hands sharply, the leopard sprang away into the thickets, making absolutely no sound as it melted into the shadows.

I had disturbed the animal in its quest for food. But a little later I heard the quickening cry of a barking deer as it fled through the forest. The hunt was still on.

The leopard, like other members of the cat family, is nearing extinction in India, and I was surprised to find one so close to Mussoorie. Probably the deforestation that had been taking place in the surrounding hills had driven the deer into this green valley; and the leopard, naturally, had followed.

It was some weeks before I saw the leopard again, although I was often aware of its presence. A dry, rasping cough sometimes gave it away. At times I felt almost certain that I was being followed.

Once, when I was late getting home, and the brief twilight gave way to a dark, moonless night, I was startled by a family of porcupines running about in a clearing. I looked around nervously, and saw two bright eyes staring at me from a thicket. I stood still, my heart banging away against my ribs. Then the eyes danced away, and I realized that they were only fireflies.

In May and June, when the hills were brown and dry, it was always cool and green near the stream, where ferns and maidenhair and long grasses continued to thrive.

Downstream I found a small pond where I could bathe, and a cave with water dripping from the roof, the water spangled gold and silver in the shafts of sunlight that pushed through the slits in the cave roof.

"He maketh me to lie down in green pastures: he leadeth me beside the still waters." Perhaps David had discovered a similar paradise when he wrote those words; perhaps I, too, would write good words. The hill station's summer visitors had not discovered this haven of wild and green things. I was beginning to feel that the place belonged to me, that dominion was mine.

The stream had at least one other regular visitor, a spotted forktail, and though it did not fly away at my approach it became restless if I stayed too long, and then it would move from boulder to boulder uttering a long complaining cry.

I spent an afternoon trying to discover the bird's nest, which I was certain contained young, because I had seen the forktail carrying grubs in her bill. The problem was that when the bird flew upstream I had difficulty in following her rapidly enough, as the rocks were sharp and slippery.

Eventually I decorated myself with bracken fronds and, after slowly making my way upstream, hid myself in the hollow stump of a tree at a spot where the forktail often disappeared. I had no intention of robbing the bird: I was simply curious to see its home.

By crouching down, I was able to command a view of a small stretch of the stream and the sides of the ravine; but I

had done little to deceive the forktail, who continued to object strongly to my presence so near her home.

I summoned up my reserves of patience and sat perfectly still for about 10 minutes. The forktail quietened down. Out of sight, out of mind. But where had she gone? Probably into the walls of the ravine where, I felt sure, she was guarding her nest.

I decided to take her by surprise, and stood up suddenly, in time to see not the forktail on her doorstep, but the leopard bounding away with a grunt of surprise! Two urgent springs, and it had crossed the stream and plunged into the forest.

I was as astonished as the leopard, and forgot all about the forktail and her nest. Had the leopard been following me again? I decided against this possibility. Only man-eaters follow humans, and, as far as I knew, there had never been a man-eater in the vicinity of Mussoorie.

During the monsoon the stream became a rushing torrent,

bushes and small trees were swept away, and the friendly murmur of the water became a threatening boom. I did not visit the place too often, as there were leeches in the long grass.

One day I found the remains of a barking deer which had only been partly eaten. I wondered why the leopard had not hidden the rest of his meal, and decided that it must have been disturbed while eating.

Then, climbing the hill, I met a party of hunters resting beneath the oaks. They asked me if I had seen a leopard. I said I had not. They said they knew there was a leopard in the forest.

Leopard skins, they told me, were selling in Delhi at over 1,000 rupees each. Of course there was a ban on the export of skins, but they gave me to understand that there were ways and means . . . I thanked them for their information and walked on, feeling uneasy and disturbed.

The hunters had seen the carcass of the deer, and they had seen the leopard pug-marks, and they kept coming to the forest. Almost every evening I heard their guns banging away, for they were ready to fire at almost anything.

"There's a leopard about," they always told me. "You should carry a gun."

"I don't have one," I said.

There were fewer birds to be seen, and even the langurs had moved on. The red fox did not show itself; and the pine martens, who had become bold, now dashed into hiding at my approach. The smell of one human is like the smell of any other.

And then the rains were over and it was October; I could lie in the sun, on sweet smelling grass, and gaze up through a pattern of oak leaves into a blinding blue heaven. And I would praise God for leaves and grass and the smell of things, the smell of mint and bruised clover, and the touch of things – the touch of grass and air and sky, the touch of the sky's blueness.

I thought no more of the men. My attitude towards them

was similar to that of the denizens of the forest. These were men, unpredictable, and to be avoided if possible.

On the other side of the ravine rose Pari Tibba, Hill of the Fairies: a bleak, scrub-covered hill where no one lived.

It was said that in the previous century Englishmen had tried building their houses on the hill, but the area had always attracted lightning, due either to the hill's location or to its mineral deposits; after several houses had been struck by lightning, the settlers had moved on to the next hill, where the town now stands.

To the hillmen it is Pari Tibba, haunted by the spirits of a pair of ill-fated lovers who perished there in a storm; to others it is known as Burnt Hill, because of its scarred and stunted trees.

One day, after crossing the stream, I climbed Pari Tibba – a stiff undertaking, because there was no path to the top and I had to scramble up a precipitous rock face with the help of rocks and roots that were apt to come loose in my groping hand.

But at the top was a plateau with a few pine trees, their upper branches catching the wind and humming softly. There I found the ruins of what must have been the houses of the first settlers – just a few piles of rubble, now overgrown with weeds, sorrel, dandelions and nettles.

As I walked through the roofless ruins, I was struck by the silence that surrounded me, the absence of birds and animals, the sense of complete desolation.

The silence was so absolute that it seemed to be ringing in my ears. But there was something else of which I was becoming increasingly aware: the strong feline odour of one of the cat family.

I paused and looked about. I was alone. There was no movement of dry leaf or loose stone. The ruins were for the most part open to the sky. Their rotting rafters had collapsed, jamming together to form a low passage like the entrance to a mine; and this dark cavern seemed to lead down into the ground.

The smell was stronger when I approached this spot, so I stopped again and waited there, wondering if I had discovered the lair of the leopard, wondering if the animal was now at rest after a night's hunt.

Perhaps he was crouching there in the dark, watching me, recognizing me, knowing me as the man who walked alone in the forest without a weapon.

I like to think that he was there, that he knew me, and that he acknowledged my visit in the friendliest way: by ignoring me altogether.

Perhaps I had made him confident – too confident, too careless, too trusting of the human in his midst. I did not venture any further; I was not out of my mind. I did not seek physical contact, or even another glimpse of that beautiful sinewy body, springing from rock to rock. It was his trust I wanted, and I think he gave it to me.

But did the leopard, trusting one man, make the mistake

of bestowing his trust on others? Did I, by casting out all fear – my own fear, and the leopard's protective fear – leave him defenseless?

Because next day, coming up the path from the stream, shouting and beating drums, were the hunters. They had a long bamboo pole across their shoulders, and slung from the pole, feet up, head down, was the lifeless body of the leopard, shot in the neck and in the head.

"We told you there was a leopard!" they shouted, in great good humour. "Isn't he a fine specimen?"

"Yes," I said. "He was a beautiful leopard."

I walked home through the silent forest. It was very silent, almost as though the birds and animals knew that their trust had been violated.

I remembered the lines of a poem by D. H. Lawrence; and, as I climbed the steep and lonely path to my home, the words beat out their rhythm in my mind: "There was room in the world for a mountain lion and me."

AMY JOHNSON,
QUEEN OF THE AIR

GORDON SNELL

In Jason *a primitive Gypsy Moth aeroplane without even a radio, Amy Johnson broke the 1930 record with her flight from England to India. Then she flew on to Australia . . .*

KARACHI WAS another of the Imperial Airways aerodromes, like Baghdad, and their officials told her to be a wise girl, and rest for a day while they overhauled her plane. But she was determined to press on, and after a lot of persuading, they agreed to work on it overnight.

Next morning, as Amy prepared to leave, there was a farewell ceremony at the aerodrome, and she had garlands put round her neck and was presented with a bouquet. An RAF plane and one from the De Havilland Company escorted *Jason* for the first part of the journey towards her next stop, Allahabad.

Strong headwinds upset her calculations, and when she landed at what she thought was Allahabad, she was still 200 miles away, at a place called Jhansi. When she realized this, she took off again at once, but after an hour's flying, her petrol was getting low, and the daylight was starting to fade, so she was forced to turn back to Jhansi again.

She landed there on the largest space she could find, which turned out to be a military parade-ground. *Jason* ran across it, and collided with a post on the far side, damaging the front edge of one wing. A carpenter from the nearby village was able to do an excellent repair job on it, while the tailor patched and sewed the wing.

Amy was helped with her engine overhaul by officers of the regiment whose parade-ground she had landed on. After a while they saw she was very tired, and brought out a camp-bed which they put beside the plane. She was able to relax on this and direct operations, while servants came to and fro from the barracks with long, cool drinks. She said it was the nicest possible way to overhaul an engine!

She was able to get enough petrol at Jhansi to fly on early the next morning to Allahabad, where she was reported as saying, as she jumped out of the plane: "40 gallons, please! I'm in a hurry to go on!" And on she went, for another 460 miles, flying into strong head winds and reaching Calcutta at six o'clock in the evening of Monday, May 12th.

She looked tired, and her face was sunburned and starting to peel, but she told reporters that she felt very fit, although she had been having only three hours sleep a night, and living mostly on a diet of sandwiches and fruit, which she ate while she was flying.

What she did want was some clean clothes to borrow – and everywhere she stopped people were happy to give her shirts and shorts, and even dresses. It was just as well, because clean clothes became quite a problem: when the front petrol tank was filled, it often overflowed, and the petrol ran into the cockpit where some of Amy's clothes were stored. The result was that she sometimes had to go to bed in petrol-soaked pyjamas, laying out the rest of her things to dry overnight.

But clothes were a minor problem indeed, compared with what Amy had to face after she left Calcutta on Tuesday morning to fly the 650 miles to Rangoon in Burma. There was monsoon weather all along the route, with high winds and driving rain – it was the worst weather she had ever experienced, and she struggled for hours to get *Jason* through it. She could hardly see anything and, after crossing the coast of Burma, she was flying low to try to get a better view.

Suddenly, she saw a 12,000-foot-high range of mountains straight ahead. She managed to turn the plane away from them, and then fly around, gaining the height she needed to get across. After that, with visibility again appalling, she came down low once more, and started to follow the railway line towards Rangoon. The airfield at Rangoon was also used as a race-course, and when she thought she saw it, Amy came thankfully in to land.

Unfortunately her landing place was actually the playing-fields of an Engineering Institute at the jungle town of Insein, ten miles north of Rangoon. *Jason* ran smoothly past the goal-posts, crashed into a wire fence, and ended up nose-down in a three-foot ditch, with the propeller broken, one of the wings smashed, a tyre ripped open, and the undercarriage damaged.

It looked like the end of *Jason*'s journey, and Amy was in tears as she climbed out of the plane. The principal of the Institute and his wife, Mr and Mrs Shaw, brought Amy into their house and gave her some clean clothes; she had a bath and a meal, and then they went, carrying huge umbrellas, out into the rainy night, to look at *Jason*. They had to cross the field which was like a sea of mud: mud which probably saved the plane from an even worse crash, by slowing it down a bit.

Though it was night-time, it was very hot, and the air was alive with insects. By the light of lamps and torches, a big crowd of local people and students from the Institute lifted *Jason* across the ditch and wheeled the plane to a more sheltered spot under some trees. Amy was in despair as she saw just how much damage there was – but Mr Shaw said cautiously that he couldn't promise anything, but he thought something could be done . . .

Next morning, he got everyone at the Institute working to help Amy, and a lot of people from the surrounding district too. The spare propeller was untied from the side of the plane, and put on instead of the broken one. The students straightened out the bent metal, and made new bolts, struts and fittings. A local rubber company representative got the tyre repaired. A Forestry Inspector gathered up the broken ribs of the wing, and glued them together like a jigsaw puzzle, to see exactly what their shape and size was. Then he got some timber and made exact copies. But there was no aeroplane fabric to cover the wing, and none of the special glue called 'Dope', used to stretch and harden the fabric. A chemist from Rangoon was able to mix a glue very like the real thing, after merely sniffing the smell from an empty tin of it.

The fabric was more of a problem – until someone remembered that over ten years ago, after the First World War, there had been a big batch of spare aeroplane fabric sold off cheaply in Rangoon, and much of it had been made into shirts. A search was made in the cupboards, and several piles of these shirts were found and brought out. They were torn into strips, and sewn together by local sewing-girls.

As well as all this, the engine had to be overhauled and cleaned again, after the coating of mud had got on to it in the ditch, and the new wing had to be fitted.

People worked in relays, carrying on all that day, through the night, and on into the next day. The heat was stifling, even during the night; the rain poured down in torrents the whole time, and the flying insects were around in such hordes that the people working had to have others standing beside them whose only job was to wave the insects away.

By late afternoon on the second day, Thursday, all the repairs were finished, and it was decided to tow *Jason* the twelve miles to Rangoon race-course, ready for take-off the next day. The local fire-engine was brought, and *Jason*'s tail was tied to the back of it. A policeman with a huge umbrella went ahead on a bicycle to clear the road, as the strange procession moved along at walking pace, stopping every 15 minutes to give the tyres a chance to cool down. The rain went on pouring down as darkness fell, and the procession continued its stately progress, lit by flaming torches that fizzed and spluttered in the wet. It took three hours to reach the race-course.

Amy was back there early the next morning, on May 16th, looking full of health and energy, wearing her socks rolled down over her shoes, as usual, and khaki shorts, a white sweater, and a raincoat. She certainly needed the raincoat, because every ten minutes there were downpours of drenching monsoon rain, followed by bright sunshine.

It was raining so heavily when she finally

took off, that when she turned to wave farewell to the people at the airfield she couldn't even see them. Visibility was still bad as she crossed the Gulf of Martaban, much feared by pilots because of its treacherous weather. Once across that, she approached the mountain range that lay across the path to her next destination, Bangkok.

She knew there was a pass through the mountains at a place called Moulmein, but after half an hour flying around and peering through the cloud and rain, she still couldn't locate it. She decided to fly up to 10,000 feet and then try to get across. There was a lot of cloud at that height, and whenever it cleared a little, she started to descend – but each time there were still mountains down below. At last she did get down through a gap in the clouds, and was delighted to see a river. Flying lower, she realized it was the river that flowed down to the sea near Moulmein: she was still on the wrong side of the mountain range!

She climbed once more to 10,000 feet, through the soaking clouds, and flew blind in what she hoped was the right direction; and she was eventually rewarded by the sight of the plains on the far side of the range. It had taken her three hours to get across those mountains – a journey that should normally have taken only half an hour.

Amy reached Bangkok aerodome at 6.30 p.m., and was welcomed by a crowd of about 1,000 Siamese. After nine hours flying in those appalling conditions, she had a terrible headache, and went to get a little rest, while the airport

mechanics began to overhaul her plane. She joined them later on, and it was a long job: for one thing, there were language problems, particularly with technical words, and for another, there was no lighting in the hangar, and they had to work by the light of Amy's small torch.

Jason was in the air again soon after dawn the next morning, with good weather for a couple of hundred miles; but then the storms came on again. This was the worst weather yet, and it lasted for 250 miles of flying. The only thing Amy could do was to keep very low, sometimes down to 50 feet, so that she could see the coastline, and follow it southwards. The rain was like a solid sheet of water, and she could see nothing through her flying goggles – so she took them off, and flew with her head out over the side of the cockpit, her stinging eyes feeling as if they were being torn out of her head.

For five hours she flew like that, following every twist and turn of the coastline. Once, she went astray and discovered she wasn't over the coast at all, but was flying round and round above some flooded fields. Finally she got through the rain, and after flying another 50 miles she landed at Singora just before three in the afternoon of Saturday, May 17th. She realized it was too late to go on to Singapore that day, so she immediately began overhauling the aircraft.

The airfield at Singora had no hangars, and was little more than a stretch of tarmac beside a sandy seashore: sand blew about constantly as Amy worked, and the tools got scorching hot in the sun.

The police roped off the area around *Jason*, which was just as well, because the local people regarded Amy and her plane as great entertainment, and there was soon a crowd of people sitting around with picnics, chattering and pointing and laughing happily. When Amy needed help with a particularly tight nut or screw, a strong man was found in the crowd to help her. Whenever she needed him she called out: "Where is the strong man?" and the crowd got to know the words. After that, when she looked round for help, they all shouted: "Strong man! Strong man!" and hooted with laughter. It was such a merry scene that Amy couldn't help laughing herself, which delighted the crowd even more.

The people came back in even greater numbers next morning to watch Amy take off. There seemed to be thousands of them: chattering men and women, Buddhist priests in long bright yellow robes, and hordes of children laughing and playing. They were standing in rows six or eight deep, on each side of the runway, almost like human hedges. Police were trying to keep the crowds back, but the children in the front kept edging forward, determined not to miss the fun. Not far from the end of the runway were some houses and a row of tall trees. It was going to be a difficult take-off . . .

After a lot of arguing and coaxing, the people were persuaded to move back a little, but there was still only a narrow path for *Jason* to move along. Any slight swerve to right or left would send the plane plunging into the crowd. Fearful of what could happen, Amy climbed into the cockpit. As *Jason* moved forward, she leaned out of the left side of the plane and looked ahead at the runway lined with excited, smiling faces. The plane gathered speed, and just as it rose from the ground, a spray of petrol from a vent-pipe spurted straight into Amy's eyes, and for a moment she could see nothing at all. She took the plane upwards, hoping desperately that it was still on a straight course. Then, to her great relief, she saw the line of trees below her, and the crowd in the distance, waving and cheering happily. She kept turning and waving back, until they were out of sight. Then she put *Jason* on course for the 470-mile flight to Singapore.

*   *   *

That Sunday, May 18th, the weather, for once, was good to Amy, and in spite of a head wind she made good time on the journey.

She landed at Singapore just before two o'clock in the afternoon, and the crowds that greeted her at the aerodrome were quite a contrast to those who had seen her off at Singora that morning.

Many of them were European women, wearing elegant dresses of muslin, lace and chiffon in bright colours, and they waved parasols and flimsy handkerchieves as she landed. Amy's oil-stained face smiled back at them.

She was wearing khaki shorts, the coat of a man's tropical drill suit, with a purple blouse underneath it, and one of those hard tropical sun-helmets called 'solar topees'. Her face was burnt almost brick-red by the tropical sun. The group of women all clapped their hands, and one onlooker said it was such a polite and dignified welcome, you'd have thought Miss Johnson had just finished singing a song at a charity concert, rather than flying solo all the way from England in 14 days.

But meanwhile, back home, Amy was being hailed as a heroine. Congratulations came from the Prime Minister, the Director of Civil Aviation, pilots like Bert Hinkler, and hundreds of ordinary people. One London theatre even told Amy's father that they would like to put her into a stage show. It didn't matter now that delays and accidents had made it impossible for Amy to beat Hinkler's record: her cheerful courage had made her the idol of people all over the world, and in Australia, they were preparing a welcome such as had never been seen before . . .

Jason took off from Singapore at ten past six the following morning, heading for Sourabaya, in Java. Amy planned to follow a route along a chain of islands, but soon after leaving Singapore the plane was engulfed by a violent rainstorm, and she could see nothing at all. She brought the plane down lower and lower, to try and find the coastline and get her bearings – sometimes she was almost skimming the crests of the waves, with her altimeter registering the plane's height as Zero. It took her three hours to get through the storm, and to make up for lost time she decided to head out across the open sea, a more direct route than following the islands.

She finally crossed the coast of Java at 4.30 p.m., over ten hours after leaving Singapore. Darkness would be falling before long – and in that part of the world, near the Equator, there is no twilight.

There wasn't time now to reach Sourabaya, so Amy headed for a nearer town called Semarang. Then she discovered that she was nearly running out of petrol – she made a forced landing on the most likely open space she could see, which turned out to be the grounds of a sugar factory at Tjomal. Unfortunately there were some bamboo stakes sticking out of the ground in the path of the plane, and their sharp ends ripped into the wings. When Amy clambered out, she found that there were five holes, each about eight inches across, in the wing fabric.

The manager and employees of the sugar factory, who

had gathered round, wondered how they could help. Then someone suggested sticking plaster. The First Aid cupboard was raided, and *Jason* really began to look as if he'd been in the wars, as strips of plaster were stuck on his wings to patch them up.

The next problem was fuel. The factory had no aeroplane fuel, but they did have some motor spirit. Amy took it gratefully, and carefully poured it into the tank, through two layers of chamois leather, to act as a filter. Even a drop of water or a grain of dirt could choke the fuel jet in the engine, and there were many stories of forced landings caused like that.

Amy stayed that Monday night at the manager's house, and next morning she faced the problem of taking off again in the restricted space, without spearing *Jason*'s wings a second time on the sharp bamboo. Fortunately there was a slightly larger field not far away, and *Jason* was pushed along to that. Amy took off successfully at 8.45 a.m., and flew to Semarang, where she landed to refuel.

She was surprised and touched by the warm welcome she got, from both aerodrome officials and the public, but what pleased her most was the generous praise of the pilots stationed there.

They told her that there were two airports at Sourabaya, where she was heading, and the right one was difficult to find – so they suggested that she should follow a Dutch air mail plane which was about to fly there. The pilot of the three-engined plane said he would go as slowly as possible so that she could keep up. But when they were airborne, she found it very hard to match his speed.

They were flying above the clouds, and Amy knew that down below there were mountains and volcanoes, so she was determined not to lose her guide – even though it meant that she had to fly at 100 miles an hour, the whole way. When she landed at Sourabaya, the engine began to splutter, and the propeller stopped dead. *Jason* came to a stop, like a runner who flops down exhausted after an all-out race.

The propeller they put on at Insein was looking very much the worse for wear after battling through the heavy monsoon rains, and Amy was worried whether it could stand up to any more strain. Someone contacted a local man with a Moth plane. He promptly sent his own propeller to be fixed to *Jason*.

The airport mechanic who was overhauling Amy's plane worked all night on it, and she arrived before dawn to test the engine. It was still spluttering. Repairs and replacements were made, but it all took so long that there was no chance of doing any flying that day. At least Amy was able to catch up on her sleep, wash her hair, and get her clothes washed.

At dawn the next morning, Thursday, May 22nd, she took off to fly the 750 miles to Atamboea, on Timor Island. The sun was shining and the world looked beautiful, and Amy flew along, singing from sheer joy. At half past eleven in the morning, she was seen flying over Sumbawa Island, nearly half-way to her destination. At Atamboea they waited to greet her. They peered at the sky until darkness fell, but there was no sign of *Jason*, and no news of her coming down anywhere else.

For nearly 24 hours Amy's family and friends, the newspapers, and people all over the world waited for news. There were fears that she had plunged into the sea she always dreaded – the Timor Sea, with its sharks.

In fact she was safe – but only just. She had flown on towards Timor Island, and reached the final stretch of over 100 miles across open sea. Darkness was approaching when she finally spotted the coast, but she still had to find Atamboea. Below her there were mountains, 9,000 feet high; she climbed high above them, peering down and trying to see an airfield – but there was no sign of one. There didn't seem to be any flat piece of ground at all, where she could land. She flew round in circles, feeling very lonely indeed, and wondering if this was to be the end of her journey, with *Jason* crashing down into those jagged mountains, never to be found.

At last she saw a clearing, and brought *Jason* down bumpily, on rough ground scattered with stunted bushes and ant-hills.

She sighed with relief as she climbed out of the plane, but the relief turned to fright, as she heard shouts, and saw dozens of men rushing towards her, waving spears and knives. They surrounded the aeroplane, talking excitedly, and Amy wondered what they were going to do. Then a big man, who seemed to be a leader, smiled at her and made a gesture of salute. He began talking to her, but there was only one word she could understand: the word, 'Pastor'. She realized there must be some kind of Church Mission nearby. The leading tribesman took her hand, and led her after him, through the darkness, with the others following.

They walked for miles over the hills, and came to a small church. Exhausted, Amy sat down against the wall of the porch, and in spite of the chattering going on all around her, she fell asleep. She woke suddenly when someone tugged at her arm: there in front of her was a dignified old man with a long beard, bowing low. The sight was so odd that she laughed nervously; the Pastor smiled, and the group of tribesmen gave a cheer. She shared a meal with the old man, and he was just showing her to a room when they heard the sound of a motor-horn.

It was a group of officials from the aerodrome at Atamboea; they had heard the sound of her plane, and come out to search for her. The place where she had been brought was called Haliloeli, and it was only 12 miles from Atamboea. But there had been a bush-fire at the airport recently, and the ground was burnt black, so that it looked from the air like a patch of dark scrubland. Amy realized she must have seen it, without knowing what it was.

She went back with the airport people to stay in Atamboea's only hotel, a ramshackle place with the hardest bed Amy had ever known.

The next morning she was taken back to *Jason*.

The Pastor had some drums of motor spirit in a shed near his church, and they had to be brought over the hills by donkey to where *Jason* was. When they arrived, Amy tried for an hour to get the petrol to go through her chamois leather filters into the tank, but without success.

Amy decided she would just have to hope that the small amount of petrol left in the tank would get her as far as Atamboea. First, some kind of flat stretch of ground had to be made, for take-off, and the villagers attacked the great ant-hills with knives and swords. Then there was a further problem: Amy didn't want to waste petrol getting the engine revved up by taxying around. She wanted the tribesmen to hold the plane in position while she revved up, then let go when she gave the signal.

They eventually understood, and got hold of the struts and the tail. But as soon as Amy opened the throttle a bit, and the engine got louder, they let go of the plane and rushed away in fright. She climbed out of the cockpit and persuaded them to come back, trying hard to explain in sign language that the engine was meant to get louder, and they would come to no harm if they held the plane until she signalled. They seemed to understand – but once again, when the throttle opened, they all fled away. Not until the fourth time did they hold on long enough for Amy to get the engine up to sufficient power. The plane rushed across the clearing and took off, just clearing the trees.

It was a short but an anxious flight to Atamboea, and there proved to be just enough petrol in the tank.

Atamboea aerodrome was really just a field, with no hangars and no proper facilities. At least there was petrol, but it was in huge drums that had been standing about for so long they were covered in red rust. When the petrol was poured out, it collected rust on the way. To make sure no rust got into the engine, Amy had first to filter the petrol from the drums into smaller tins, and then filter it from those, through her chamois leather, into the tank. There was another worry – the oil supplies that were supposed to

be waiting at Atamboea had not come through. She had only one spare gallon with her, and she just had to add that to the half gallon or so of dirty oil that was left in the sump of the engine.

There was not time, now, to set off for Darwin so Amy decided to spend the rest of the day giving *Jason*'s engine a thorough overhaul. She checked every pipe and every joint for any sign of leakage, put in new plugs, and tightened up every single nut and bolt on the engine and on the plane.

It was a fine morning, cool and fresh, on Saturday, May 24th, when Amy took off, just before eight o'clock. The engine hummed along merrily, as *Jason* flew over a calm sea, and Amy kept thinking happily: "Australia soon! Australia soon!" The dangers and disappointments of the past days now seemed like bad dreams. The flight was so smooth that time seemed to slow down – Amy would look at the clock, thinking half an hour had gone by, and discover it was only ten minutes. Then, down below, she sighted the oil tanker *Phorus*, which had been sent to the midway point of her course, just in case she was in any trouble. She swooped down and flew low over it, flinging a cake at one of the people standing on deck. The crew cheered, and Amy flew on, thinking how the ship's wireless operator would be even now sending out the signal to the world, saying she was nearing her final destination.

The next hour passed quickly, as *Jason* went smoothly on over the empty sea. Then time seemed to drag again: would Australia never show up? At last Amy saw land: Melville Island, a landmark she'd been looking out for, not far off the Australian coast. As she looked down on the surf breaking on the island's shore, she slapped *Jason*'s sides, and rocked about in her seat, cheering loudly. Then, as she neared the mainland, she picked up the air-cushion she had inflated, to keep her afloat if she should crash into the Timor Sea. She thumped it, yelling with delight, and then threw it over the side.

She crossed the coast and was about to look around for the aerodrome when she saw two planes ahead, waiting to escort her in. She flew between them, and saw the crowds around the airfield, gazing upwards, waiting to welcome her. Suddenly the tears came to her eyes: it was true – she had done what she set out to do, and here she was, Amy Johnson, alone in her little Gipsy Moth, *Jason*, actually landing in Australia!

NO PICNIC ON MOUNT KENYA

FELICE BENUZZI

Felice, Giuàn and Enzo were bored with being prisoners in a British camp in Central Africa so they decided to break out and climb Mount Kenya, 17,000 feet high. They had to make their own equipment, and had very little information about the two peaks, Batian and Lenana, or of other features of the mountain, whose names occur in the story.

At 11 a.m. we were at last attacking the rocks at the foot of Petit Gendarme, in other words the very body of Batian.

The first rope-lengths were rather easy although the rocks were rotten and offered no sound belay. Soon we met much damp snow, covered now and then with a thin frozen crust. At every belay I left an arrow.

First we kept trying to swing to the left in the direction of the gap, our immediate aim, but the rocks became smoother and soon they offered no holds at all. Thus we climbed vertically, hoping to find higher up a traverse to the left.

More and more snow plastered the slabs. Had it been frozen to any depth it would have offered us, in exchange for the relatively light labour of step-cutting a good and quick way up; but it was not and Giuàn had to clean it off and as I was as a rule directly below him little snow avalanches hit me regularly. If I looked up to give him another foot of rope from my belay the snow would fall on my face, and if I bent my head it landed on my neck and went under my clothes and down my spine. I comforted my-self by trying to imagine that it was an agreeable change from our camp showers, but I could not find it agreeable for all that.

A sad disappointment was the discovery that the rocks under the snow plaster appeared to be smooth slabs as

devoid of holds as those we had already decided not to try towards the gap. Presently I could give no more belay to Giuàn. We were already risking too much, or as the Italian proverb has it 'pulling the Devil by his tail'. Had Giuàn fallen he would have dragged me with him and vice-versa.

Nevertheless we continued to advance by inches, hoping to strike a possible line of traverse towards the gap or an ascent line towards the arète between the gap and the top of Petit Gendarme. It was distinctly a tough struggle. In some places I was able to leave an arrow, fixing it with a piece of snow-crust. After all, we had to consider our return-journey.

I wondered if we had reached 5,000 metres, which would have been an achievement in itself for every Alpine climber as the highest peak of the Alps, Mount Blanc itself, is only 4,807 metres.

Giuàn was faced with a peculiarly awkward pitch and the minutes dragged on into a quarter of an hour without any appreciable gain. My fingers were already numbed with cold. I managed to move the ropes, which were our very theoretical safeguard, only with great difficulty.

At 12.30 p.m., to my horror, I noticed ràgs of mists coming from the south. In no time they enveloped the upper part of north-west ridge, while other tongues blown by an increasingly strong wind passed through the gap we had so far failed to reach and condensed on our side of the mountain. Soon they enveloped Northey and César Glaciers, Dutton Peak, 'Black Tooth', everything.

The temperature dropped. An ice storm brought more and more misty clouds. I started shivering. Giuàn's ghostly grey figure alternately disappeared and reappeared on the rocks above my head.

He seemed unable to advance. He too was probably considering the situation from this new point of view.

"Hello!" I shouted to him.

"Hello!" came his answer, half drowned by the whistling of the wind.

"How are you going on?"

"Not at all."

I didn't answer.

"I see no possibility," he carried on after a while, "of going an inch further, nor perhaps of getting back." I still do not know – and neither does he – how he had managed to climb as far as he had.

I cannot remember the exact words we shouted to each other in the roar of the storm, but it was a very short conversation which, as a novelist would say, "held life and death in the balance".

We decided to retreat, if possible.

While Giuàn, inch by inch, made his sorrowful and awkward way down the temperature seemed to me to rise again, and it started snowing and hailing together. Not only would any attempt to climb further have been unpardonable lunacy, but the prospects of a safe retreat began to appear rather problematic.

For the following forty minutes – and it took Giuàn that long to reach the spot where I still clung to the rock – the storm was dead against us. Slowly my numbed fingers, cut and bruised during the past week by bamboo and rock, retrieved the rope which separated me from my friend. Fortunately the wind was so strong that the falling snow did not immediately cover the rocks. Had it done so the red arrows I had left would have been hidden and we should have been hopelessly lost.

When Giuàn joined me at last on my precarious perch his eyebrows, moustaches and blanket-suit were frozen with ice and his lips were almost white. According to my reading, people in similar circumstances shake hands. We had neither the inclination nor the time to do so at that moment.

The wind dropped a little but the snow fell more steadily and more thickly. Snow-flakes whirled round us, snow heaped on every irregularity of the rocks and plastered the wool of our caps, jackets and trousers with an icy crust.

Thus we started the descent, doubly difficult as we were

retracing our steps not only because of the blizzard but also owing to the fact that we had been 'technically' defeated by the rocks.

Clinging to my small holds I peered down into the fury of the elements, trying to locate a red arrow in all this white hell. At last I saw one, a welcome sign of life in this dead world. Slowly and with great effort we reached it. "Shall we have the strength to attempt Lenana tomorrow in order to hoist our flag there at last?" I asked myself. "Shall we be able to descend from Batian today?" was the question I was afraid to ask myself.

(With great difficulty they struggle back to their tiny tent, their last scraps of food, and a day of exhausted rest.)

February 6th

It was 1 a.m. when we got up after only a few hours of sleep. On the last flickering flame of the boiler Enzo melted the lump of ice which had formed in the cooking pot. When

the water was just getting warm the flame died out. The alcohol was finished.

In the warm water Enzo washed the inner side of the bags which had contained Ovaltine, powdered milk and cocoa, added the four tea-spoons of sugar, a few leaves of tea and served it almost cold.

It proved a delightful mixture. In addition we had one biscuit each and the last of the meat-extract.

At 1.50 a.m. Giuàn and I started. The torch cast a dim failing light, perfect symbol of the strength of our party.

The night seemed to me colder than the one preceding our attempt on Batian, and if the same rules as regards weather were applicable to Kenya as in the Alps, this presaged a fine day.

Though we had started one and a quarter hours earlier than on 'Batian day' we only reached the lower tarn at 3 a.m. We lost our way several times among the boulders, and after having made a longer detour between the two tarns owing to the weak light shed by our torch, we arrived at the upper tarn only forty minutes earlier than on the previous day.

We were amazed when we saw the whole surface of the tarn covered with ice. In the light of the stars it was a wonderful sight. More wonderful, although not entirely necessary as we were not at all thirsty, was the new experience which followed. With the point of our ice-axes we opened a hole in the ice and, lying on the smooth surface, we sucked a drink of water through the hole.

The ascent of the steep slope below 'Molar Saddle' was particularly hard. To avoid repeating the error made as we came down from Batian when we found ourselves in a ravine on the left side of the valley, I erred in the opposite direction, as happens not only while mountaineering. We struck so far to the right that we finished on the front moraine of Joseph Glacier.

As soon as we became aware of my new mistake, we climbed down a steep gorge and up the far side to the scree.

This new waste of time upset us thoroughly. We wanted to reach the top of Lenana at 10 a.m., as on the day before the storm on the peaks had started at this hour and we feared that it might repeat itself.

Scarcely had we started up the scree when the torch decided to call it a day and the fading light died out completely. In pitchblack darkness we scrambled on, often sliding down several yards in the attempt to make one step up.

It was a long tiring job, and we were very relieved to reach the 'Molar' at last. From the cache I produced the crampons and ropes and slowly we started descending the side of Mackinder's Valley. The stars shone brightly giving us some light, but as neither of us had been here before we had to conduct this night march on *terra incognita* with care.

There was a nip in the air which pierced the very bones. We were over 15,000 feet up and it was the hour before dawn, the coldest of the night.

The sky was clear; the Southern Cross hung glorious over Point Piggott and Magellan's Cloud was setting on the western horizon, but not even from this altitude could we see the Polar Star.

We reached two little pools on the moraine of Northey Glacier. Beyond them the ground proved rocky and we thought it better to sit down and to await daylight.

By and by the gloomy fore-castle of the *Flying Dutchman* grew paler and paler and round the pools we could distinguish the lobelias, looking in the first dim light of day like funerary torches or stones in an Arab cemetery.

At last the sky between Sendeyo and Lenana blushed rosy. There was no breath of wind. An abysmal silence reigned.

Always, and more especially on mountains, have I watched daybreak with deep awe. It is an age-old miracle which repeats itself again and again, every day the same and every day different. It is the hour of Genesis.

Then, on the high bowsprit of the *Flying Dutchman* there rose a flag of flame-colour, while her petrified bulwarks showed faintly rose. A breeze passed over the rocks and rippled the surface of the pools slightly.

It was day and we could start marching again.

The morning was glorious and as we walked straight toward the rising sun the whole of Mackinder's Valley was bathed in golden light.

The curled pinnacle near the summit of Lenana twinkling on the horizon above the violet-shaded Gregory glacier looked cheerful and inviting.

We passed close to the foot of the formidable-looking north-east ridge, making our way between boulders of all sizes and shapes. I particularly remember one of them of the exact size and shape of a grand piano.

On our left the valley got narrower and at its head we saw the unbroken blue-green mirror of a tarn. The brook formed by its outlet roared down the valley, recalling to my memory the noises, as of another world, made by trains which run through some Alpine valleys.

Frequently we looked at the western face of Sendeyo (our *Flying Dutchman*) not yet touched by the sun and appearing gloomy and terrible, and wondered if ever a bold climber had scaled those fascinating rocks from this side.

We did our best to keep along one contour at the base of the north-eastern face of Batian, but soon we realized that we should have to lose some height as one of the pillars supporting the gigantic walls had its base below our altitude. While descending slightly we could not help being attracted by the features of this north-east wall. It was still virgin ground as no party had managed to reach Batian's summit from this side. Only on July 31st, 1944 did Arthur H. Firmin, Nairobi, and Peter Hicks, Eldoret, in a brilliant climb make the first ascent of the north-east face.

Dutton compared this sight to gigantic organ-pipes. I, not having read Dutton's book at this time, recalled a forlorn valley-top under the sheer 4,000-feet drop of the west face of Jof Fuart in the western Julian Alps, where from time immemorial the herdsmen had called a place like this '*lis altaris'*: 'the altars'. Not by mere chance is the mountain climber induced to think of organ-pipes or of altars as he looks up those towering rocks; it is a religious feeling which fills his heart.

As we reached the edge of the buttress which had forced us to lose height we found ourselves facing another little marvel, recalling homely mountain customs. At almost a man's height the rock showed a niche, rounded as though carved by man's tools. At the foot of the niche and round it, the rock was covered by helichrysums clinging in a compact cushion and enjoying the sun. One could hardly believe that the flowers had grown there spontaneously; they seemed to have been put there, in homage to an invisible Madonna in a wayside shrine, by some wanderer who saw in the majesty of the mountain a sign of the Creator's might.

Gaining height again we set foot on the moraine of a small glacier bearing the name of the discoverer of Mount Kenya, Krapf. Later we crossed the scree which comes down from Point Thomson and soon found a large, almost horizontal ledge of rocks, partially split by ravines and resembling an ancient road. It led straight to a flat saddle which I think is Flake Col, although on Dutton's map it bears no name at all.

We did not make for the col but scrambled up easy, partially ice-covered rocks, aiming toward the ridge of Lenana itself. Only our desire to be on the summit of Lenana by ten o'clock lent us speed. We felt very weak and every step was a real effort.

At 8 a.m., six hours after leaving the base camp, we were on the top of the ridge. We sat down, basking in the sun and finishing the contents of our 'climbing-bag', crumbs of chocolate, toffee and sultanas.

We were generously compensated for the lack of food by the magnificent view. At our feet lay Nithy Valley between two gentle slopes dotted with rocks and groundsels and showing several shimmering pools.

Further down we noticed the Hall tarns glittering with water and the clear-cut drop above the dark-green lake

Michaelson; further on a seemingly boiling sea of clouds cloaked the plains, but two dark ridges protruded looking like whales among the waves. I believe they were Mount Ithungani and Mount Fangani. Almost at the uttermost limit of vision on the north-eastern horizon rose a black table-topped mountain such as may be seen commonly in Ethiopia. We wondered if it was Marsabit, the paradise of big game hunters.

The eastern face of Batian presented a totally different but an equally beautiful sight. It was an unbelievable bright yellow ochre in colour. Any painter portraying it would be blamed for exaggeration, but perhaps no painter in the world could reproduce *this* yellow.

After a short pause for resting and sketching, we followed the crest towards the summit. The rock has a reddish colour totally different from Batian, and its 'behaviour' in so far as this affects the climber is quite different as well. On Batian's north side we had found on the whole solid, reliable rock, sometimes even too smooth. Lenana had craggy rotten rock. As soon as the climber grasps it whole vertical slabs tend to break away with a slight pull . . .

Once we had reached Lenana's 'handle' we tried to circumvent it from the glacier side, but we were so weary that we found the rocks too difficult and had to make a little detour to the east. Here we should have found, according to Dutton's map, Kolbe Glacier; but owing to the general retreat of all glaciers on Kenya, as well as on Kilimanjaro and Ruwenzori, we did not see even a remnant of it.

By this route we reached the shoulder above the 'handle'.

Giuàn showed me some stones he had collected. They bore strange oblong crystal plates ('rhomb-porphids') looking like stamps. While he was trying to increase his new stamp-collection he noticed a pair of sun-glasses with the once white glare-refractor yellowish and weather-stained. The owner of these glasses was not popular with us. Instead of blessing him for losing something which might have been of use to us – as a rule everything is of some use to a PoW and the exceptions to this rule have still to be found – we blamed him for having lost only his glasses. Could he not have mislaid, for instance, a tin of sardines or of meat or cheese? We should have devoured it on the spot, as in the 'refrigerator' at 16,300 feet it would have kept for several years.

After advancing a few yards along the broad shoulder we saw the cairn marking the top not far from us.

I waited a while for Giuàn who was still busy collecting 'stamps' – or hoping that the owner of the glasses or someone else might have dropped something edible – and together, filled by an odd feeling almost of solemnity we reached the point where one could ascend no farther.

We shed our rucksacks and ice-axes and sat down, looking around. It was 10.05 a.m.

A great peace hung over the broad expanse. Under the dark velvety sky the wonderful scenery of the country at our feet had a strange radiance.

This was the climax of eight months' preparation and of two weeks of toil. It was worth both.

BICYCLES UP KILIMANJARO

RICHARD CRANE & NICHOLAS CRANE

*The Crane cousins climbed Kilimanjaro, nearly 20,000 feet high.
Having brought their bicycles to the top, they came down quicker than
they went up. They take turns to tell the story.*

THE IRONY OF having to carry a bicycle *down* a hill was,
even to brains which felt as if they'd been steeped in
quick-setting cement, too much to bear – as was the
weight of a velocipede and two rucksacks on bruised
shoulders.

My first attempt at high-altitude freewheeling ended in
spectacular disaster. The combined weight of rider, bike and
rucksacks was over 130 kilograms; a lot for a pair of brakes to
hold in normal conditions. I was sitting on the back rack of
the bike, keeping the weight as far rearwards as possible on
the 45° scree slope; I could just reach the handlebars with
outstretched fingers. What I didn't realize until the whole
ensemble was travelling at breakneck speed was that I
couldn't see where I was going. The rucksack I was wearing
on my chest had been pushed upwards into my face,
leaving me totally sightless as the bike reached terminal
velocity, hit a lump of lava and took off.

*(Dick) I waited till the dust had settled to see if Nick was going to
get up. He'd entirely disappeared in a great mushroom cloud.*

When it cleared, Nick was lying upside down and covered from head to foot in grit. His bike was several feet down the slope. I was already on my bike. I don't like to let a good chance to experiment with physical extremes escape me. Nick's method: feet on pedals, bum over the rear wheel, brakes on firmly, worked after a fashion, but it was hard work. My arms felt surprisingly weak after only ten feet. To impress Nick, and also to go one better, I decided to hang on until I was a few feet past him, before getting off for a rest. I took a line slightly wide of where Nick's legs were splayed out, adopted a racy pose with legs slightly bent and springy on the pedals. I just missed the knobble which had toppled Nick, but my front wheel suddenly dropped into a dip and I was over the handlebars. Rucksacks and I landed in the grit. Life was getting fun again. Here we were at 17,500 feet, playing BMX.

For several hundred feet we experimented with varying modes of downhill travel. Most ended with wild uncontrollable slides and somersaults. We looked like a couple of corporation dustcarts falling down a cliff face. Each pile-up was accompanied by fruity language, luggage breaking free and explosions of lava flour which hung in the air above the victim like bomb bursts. Dick, being annoyingly innovative as usual, was experimenting with forward-loading of luggage. He had a rucksack tied on his handlebars and another on the back, while he himself attempted to hitch a ride on the rear carrier. It proved a dramatic demonstration of the forces of gravity over friction. The bike turned over, end on end, and Dick's large expedition rucksack took off down the slope in a series of giant hops, with its owner bounding down after it shouting "Crimbals! Crimbals!"

If the mashed potato had looked unpalatable at our ice-camp, I could just imagine what it would look like after it had been atomised over the inside of a rucksack. A hundred feet below me, Dick rugby tackled his errant luggage, and the two of them slid to a dusty halt. Picking up Dick's abandoned bike, I wondered for a moment whether, with two bikes now at my disposal, I could somehow create a catamaran effect, and ride both at once down the scree. But it was just too difficult to balance. By the time I reached Dick, he had dreamt up the final solution:

(Dick) The fastest way of descending the scree was by not actually riding the bike, but using it as a wheeled outrigger. This may sound like cheating, in that it's not actually 'riding' the bike, but it turned out to be a very quick way of travelling down steep scree with a heavy load. You lie diagonally across the bike, legs out in the dirt one side, wheels churning the dust on the other. The bike's top-tube is tucked into your armpit, eyes peeking over the handlebars, and rucksacks resting on the saddle and rear rack. Following my near disaster with the disappearing rucksack, I had my two packs strapped to my bike then I strapped myself to the packs thus making a complete unit. The rear brakes are locked on, but partially released

every few yards to prevent the rubber wearing through. The front wheel is allowed to turn like a slowly revolving ski.

Although I hated to admit it, Dick's monocoque slalom theory did seem to work. We tore down a thousand feet with a speed and verve that would make Jean-Claude Killy look like a dumper-truck on a nursery slope. With every foot descended we felt better. The crippling lethargy of the past two days was lifting, though the headaches were still there, drilling away at addled grey-matter. It wasn't our legs that finally gave out during this flying finish, but a far more sensitive part; a part that had been bruised and chafed on a leather saddle for too long – our right armpits.

It was agonizing. The jarring and rubbing suddenly came home with red-hot fire and numb cries of 'Ggnnuunng'. It took a quarter of an hour to swap sides, so that we could inflict the same pain to our left armpits. One more long slalom and it was time to stop for a rest. It was nearly dark.

(Dick) We stopped breathless to gaze down scree, and back up from where we had come. All around the evening was closing in. Gloves and balaclavas came out, and we zipped up our jackets. Nick put his head-torch over his head in preparation for darkness, and I got mine ready for use by clipping the battery terminals on. Nick then took his head-torch off again, clipped on his battery terminals, and placed it back on his head. Together in spirit, although slightly out of tune with regard to the speed of our mental processes, we set off.

Our antics on the scree were being observed from below. Outside Kibo Hut Michèle and a crowd of German trekkers were following our every fall through binoculars. The entire descent is visible from below, and in the fading light they'd watched the wisps of dust rise from the dark lava.

"What are they doing?" asked a newly arrived French girl, wrapped up in a thick duvet and mittens.

"Riding bicycles," Michèle replied without looking away from the Zeiss eyepieces.

"Oh, I see." The girl moved slowly away, looking at Michèle over her shoulder, as if further contact would cause her too to start saying crazy things.

With the dusk came the cold, and the temperature slipped quickly below freezing. The watchers saw the two tiny figures halt for what seemed ages, then start out again, this time pin-pointed by two twinkling lights. Darkness wrapped itself around the mountain, and the two dots of light winked lower and lower. Somebody asked Michèle if the two cyclists would actually be riding their bikes, and she answered knowingly: "I should think so. They're mad enough to try anything!"

Up on the scree, our high spirits had evaporated with the enveloping blackness. All we could see of each other was a wildly swaying beam of light, which sometimes pointed downhill, but more often than not veered wildly into the sky or across the surrounding slopes, accompanied by a muttered curse as yet another boulder was struck. We were each isolated in our own private struggle. In the dark it was harder to share the effort, and the problems seemed to multiply. I'd now tied both my rucksacks on top of each other, and they kept swinging to one side and pulling me over. It was driving me mad, I was cold, and couldn't be bothered to stop and unship the gargantuan load which I knew would take me ten minutes to get onto my back again. When I did finally chuck it all on the ground, my hands were so cold I couldn't get the rucksack straps undone. And I discovered that two of the Karrimats that had been tied to my load, had disappeared somewhere during the descent. Dick was down below me. He too had stopped and I could see his illuminated hands also fighting a rucksack. It was impossible to tell how much further we had to go; there didn't seem to be any light at Kibo Hut.

Dick waited for me while I slithered clumsily down the scree to him. Every few feet the bike seemed to pile into a rock and stop dead and I'd end up on one or both knees trying not to fall down the slope.

"Can't be much further," was all he said.

The gradient soon eased, and more to liven things up than make quicker progress, we decided to have a go at riding the bikes. It was quite the most hair-brained idea. The head-torches picked out the rocks ahead, but our reaction times had slowed down so much that we'd be unable to avoid them. We scooted feet-down, managing a few feet-up sections once we got below the lava cliffs that stand above the Hut. Here the trail gets firmer, and we found that as long as we could control our swaying backpacks, the bikes could pick a safe line between the boulders.

(Dick's diary.) Helluva steep scree. A lot more fun coming down than going up. Rucksacks strapped to bikes. Many topples. Gravel everywhere, even in my underpants. Should be sorry to see the end of the expedition but right now I'm thankful for the back of the mountain. I hope there's Pete, Michèle and grub ready at the bottom.

Michèle had seen one light emerge at the bottom of the cliffs, and hurried over to the petrol stove, pumped it into life, and re-heated the jug of tea she'd had simmering for the past half-hour. A small knot of porters and guides had gathered in the cold at the corner of the hut, and were looking expectantly up the slope.

For us it was a wonderful moment. We found ourselves suddenly in sight of the hut's tin roof, and spurred on by its closeness we rode the last hundred yards without falling off, rounded the last bend and pedalled right into what at the time seemed a throng the size of a Cup Final crowd. People milled everywhere; there must have been nearly fifteen. Michèle bounded up bearing a huge aluminium jug in one hand and a plate of popcorn in the other. The jug was full to the brim with the best tea ever to grace parched throats.

Acknowledgements

For permission to reproduce copyright material, acknowledgement and thanks are due to the following:

Abner Stein for 'The Golden Apples of the Sun' © 1953 by Ray Bradbury; renewed 1981 by Ray Bradbury; A P Watt Ltd on behalf of The Executors of the Estate of Robert Graves for an extract (slightly abridged) from *The Golden Fleece* by Robert Graves; The Bodley Head for an extract from *The Light Beyond the Forest* by Rosemary Sutcliff; Andre Deutsch Ltd for 'Shane' by Jack Shaefer from *Shane and Other Stories*; Hamlyn Publishing Group Ltd for 'Pony Express' by Robin May from *True Adventures of the Wild West*; Macmillan, London and Basingstoke for an extract from *The Dolphin Crossing* by Jill Paton Walsh; Jonathan Clowes Ltd, London, on behalf of Doris Lessing for 'Through the Tunnel' from *The Habit of Loving*, copyright 1954 Doris Lessing; George Lamming for 'Boy Blue the Crab Catcher'; The Bodley Head for an extract from *A Hundred Million Francs* by Paul Berna, translated by John Buchanan-Brown; Penguin Books Ltd for an extract from *The Sound of Propellers* (pp. 101–116) by Clive King (Kestrel Books, London 1986), copyright © Clive King, 1986; Andre Deutsch Ltd for an extract from *Albeson and the Germans* by Jan Needle; Century Hutchinson for an extract from *Southern Cross to Pole Star* by A. F. Tschiffely; Chatto & Windus for an extract from *The Flame Trees of Thika* by Elspeth Huxley; Ruskin Bond for 'The Leopard'; William Kimber & Co Ltd for an extract from *No Picnic on Mount Kenya* by Felice Benuzzi; Oxford Illustrated Press for an extract from *Bicycles Up Kilimanjaro* by Richard Crane and Nicholas Crane.

While every effort has been made to obtain permission, there may still be cases in which we have failed to trace a copyright holder, and we would like to apologize for any apparent negligence.